SECRET *dynasty*

THE DYNASTIES
BOOK THREE

SECRET *dynasty*

GENEVA LEE

ESTATE
PUBLISHING + ENTERTAINMENT

To Jenn

CHAPTER ONE

"You are *Kerrigan Belmond.*"

The words hit me with the force of a bomb. Explosive but deadly quiet because that's what happened to the victim. They were gone before they knew what had happened. With four words, he obliterated me. It took me a moment to gather my fragmented thoughts and face him. Tears dried on my cheeks as I sat in silence, trying to think of what to say. In the end, there was only one way to respond.

"You're crazy." I stared at him, waiting for him to crack a smile or break into laughter. But he didn't.

Tod Belmond's face was cold and hard as if it were carved from stone. I thought he'd been heartless before, but now I knew it was so much worse.

I was not Kerrigan Belmond, his daughter. I was

not an heiress or a socialite. I didn't attend Oxford and vacation on the French Riviera. I was a shit waitress from West Bexby. I was an orphan. I existed. I was real. I was standing in front of him now. He couldn't just erase me.

But that was exactly what he was doing.

"My name is Kate," I said defiantly.

"Kerrigan..." His voice was rich with warning, but I didn't care.

"I'm Kate. I worked in a pub." My eyes skittered toward Iris. She was frozen, her face a mask of mute horror. I hated that she was finding out this way. "You found me and offered me money—a lot of money—to pretend to be your daughter until she returns home from wherever she ran off to."

That's how this had all started. I'd been at work when a couple of entitled pricks took a picture of me and told me I looked like Kerrigan Belmond. Tod had tracked me down the following day and explained his predicament. His daughter had run away from her privileged life, and he needed me to pretend to be her to avoid ruining her arranged marriage to Spencer Byrd, a wealthy aristocrat. I'd thought it sounded mental at the time. I still did, but it was too crazy to make up.

I turned to Tod to remind him of all of that—to remind him that this was all his idea. Our eyes met, and an icy chill ran up my spine. My argument faded into the background as we glared at each other. His lips turned down, and he shook his head. "Perhaps, you should sit down."

"No." There was only one way I was staying in this house. I wanted answers, not lies. "Where is Kerrigan?"

"I already told you that you—"

"Stop lying to me!" My head began to pound. The chill I'd felt a moment ago spread through my skin like I'd been plunged into ice water. I pressed a fingertip to my temple as my vision went fuzzy. I locked my legs and tried to fight the panic attack. Now wasn't the time to lose control. Not now. Not when I was about to get answers.

"I think it's best if we all take a moment," Iris interjected softly. She moved closer to her husband as though to take her place by his side.

She believed him. It was evident from the compassion etched in her face. Or was it just pity for the crazy girl? I wasn't sure it mattered.

I looked at her, disappointment washing through me. "You believe him..." I stuttered in shock. "Did you know he brought me here?"

There was a pause before she nodded.

Who else was playing Tod's game? What if they all believed him? Giles. Iris. Who else? The walls started to shrink, the air becoming thick and unbreathable. He'd laid a trap for me with ten million pounds as bait.

Now that he had me safely in a cage, I had nowhere to go. No one would believe me after he'd whispered all those lies. I wasn't a pawn. I was a prisoner.

And I needed to escape before it was too late.

"We should call the doctor," Tod spoke quietly to Iris, all of his attention focused on the next step in his plot.

Was that part of his plan? Tod Belmond had enough money to pay someone to say I was crazy. I was sure of that. But Iris wouldn't allow that, would she? I couldn't wait around to find out.

I stood on shaky legs and wiped a palm across my tear-stained cheeks. Lifting my head, I looked to Eliza, who hadn't spoken since the confrontation began. She'd been so quiet I nearly forgot she was here. Her dark eyes remained round as saucers, and she'd pressed herself against a wall. I couldn't imagine what she thought of this situation.

Not only did I need to get out of here, but I needed to get her out, too. Who knew what Tod might do to prevent me from ruining his plans for Kerrigan.

And that was precisely the problem. Tod Belmond had money. He had resources. He had powerful friends and private detectives. He held all the winning cards. There was no beating him. I either had to fold and go along with it or bluff.

"I'm going to Sparrow Court," I announced. "I don't want to be here." I looked at Eliza. "Do you want to come with me?"

I prayed she said yes.

But Tod drew himself up, shaking his head. "I think you should stay here, Kerrigan."

I bristled at the use of her name but didn't say anything, even though I was screaming inside. It would be a wasted effort to yell or argue. Tod had chosen his play. I was making mine.

"I told Spencer I would join him." Another lie. But if all of this were about ensuring the arrangement between the two families, Tod wouldn't want to keep me from him.

"Spencer has his hands full. He needs to attend to his family and deal with his grandfather's death. You should respect that," Tod barked at me.

"That's why I should be with him." I crossed my arms, making up my mind to see this through until he either locked me in a closet somewhere or I'd made it out the door.

Tod opened his mouth, but before he could argue, Iris placed a hand on his arm.

"You can't keep her here," Iris said.

His shoulders slumped as he looked to his wife. "What if she runs off again?"

The hollow ache in his voice was so pitch-perfect he nearly had me convinced. He deserved an award for his performance. No wonder she believed him. And if she believed him, so would everyone else.

He studied me for a moment before finally nodding. "On one condition."

"Condition?" I repeated. Now we were negotiating?

"You agree to see your doctor tomorrow," he said firmly.

A scream caught in my throat. I didn't have a doctor. He knew that. The lie was all part of his plan. But tempting as it was to fight him on this, I realized it was easier to agree. Once I walked out the front door, I could clear my head. He had control of this room and this house.

"Fine." I managed to keep my indignation to a minimum. There was no way I was meeting with some doctor on his payroll.

"Giles will go with you," he added.

"I need a chaperone now?" I planted my hands on my hips, searching for another option. I glanced at Eliza. "I'll take Eliza. She needs to meet Spencer anyway if she's going to be my maid of honor."

Bringing up the wedding was all part of my plan. The more I pretended I was going to marry Spencer, the longer my leash would be. But there wasn't going to be a wedding. I knew that. Somewhere down-deep, Tod had to know it, too.

Eliza let out a small squeak like she resented being dragged into this. I wished I had another option.

"We'll discuss that later," Tod said tightly. "But as long as you have someone with you while you're so upset."

Upset? That was the word he landed on? I was somewhere far north of upset.

"Is it a good idea for you to see Spencer right now?" Iris asked. "Perhaps, we should talk."

"I don't want to talk to you," I said coldly, and she flinched as though I'd slapped her. I had trusted Iris, but she had been lying to me since the moment we met. I knew that now. There was no one in this house I could trust, and the sooner I got out of here, the better.

"I'll call the driver," Tod said.

"I can drive," I stopped him. "I'm sure you've got all sorts of ways to track me."

When he didn't counter my assumption, I knew I was right. All of London was my cage. He could find me anywhere here. No wonder Kerrigan had run to other countries. How had she finally escaped him? Where was she now?

I ignored the tiny voice in my head that told me I knew where she was—or, I had at least narrowed it down to two possibilities. People didn't just vanish. Something had happened to her. I'd suspected that for a while. Was she dead? Locked away? A tiny voice in my head whispered there was one more possibility.

I ignored it.

I was not crazy. There had to be an explanation for all of this. I would uncover the secrets. I would find the truth. I focused on that as I grabbed Eliza's hand and dragged her toward the garage, avoiding Iris's pitying

gaze and Tod's calculated glare. It didn't matter what
he said or what she believed.

I was not Kerrigan Belmond.

Right?

CHAPTER TWO

Like most wealthy families, the Belmonds had several cars in the garage. I bypassed the Maybach, not wanting to call the driver Tod employed and not feeling like it was my right to take it. Eliza remained silent as we walked past the empty vehicles, but her eyes were wide with surprise. I understood how she felt. There was a difference in being told someone had billions and seeing it for yourself. The garage said everything that words couldn't. I paused and considered Iris's car, a sleek Mercedes, but before I could ask myself if I was angry enough with her to take it without permission, Giles shuffled in behind us. He cleared his throat casually and held out a Chanel clutch. Judging by the uncomfortable pinch to his features, he had already heard what happened.

"I assume you'll want your license and some

money," he said, taking his glasses off to wipe them on a handkerchief.

It was a surprisingly thoughtful gesture, but I knew better than to let my guard down. Giles hadn't been present for my confrontation with Tod. The fact that he was here now, suggested he'd either heard about it or been informed of the row.

"Which car is hers?" I asked him.

Giles tilted his head toward the final row in the garage toward a yellow coupe. "That one is yours."

Yours.

I did my best to ignore the implication in his words. Instead, I strode toward it, Eliza and Giles following close behind me. Kerrigan Belmond drove a canary-yellow Porsche 911. I stared at it for a moment, willing myself to remember seeing the vehicle before. If this was mine, I would remember it. Between the color and its sexy sports car lines, it wasn't the type of car that was easy to forget.

"The key fob is inside it," Giles told me. "Try not to wreck it again."

Again.

So that's how *she* drove: recklessly. Why didn't that surprise me?

"*I'm* a very safe driver," I said back to him coolly.

If Giles understood what I was really saying, he ignored it. "I doubt he'll buy you another after last time," he warned me, sticking to the charade Tod had started in his office. "When can we expect you to return?"

"Does it matter?" I snapped.

"I merely want to set up an appointment with Dr. Baker for you." He paused as if waiting for me to fight him on this.

My stomach flipped over at the thought of visiting Kerrigan's doctor. Surely, he wouldn't go along with this ploy. I could talk to him. There were codes of conduct. I could file a complaint if he wouldn't listen. I took a deep breath to steady myself. "I thought you made my schedule." I shrugged. "Whenever."

"Once we know more about the funeral, I will arrange it." His response was stiff. There was a moment's hesitation, and I half expected him to say something. Instead, he smiled tightly and left.

Eliza exhaled loudly next to me. "What the actual fuck?"

"You can say that again," I muttered. "Let's get out of here."

"No arguments from me."

I slid behind the wheel of the Porsche, tucking the small clutch next to the console. I pushed the ignition button. It roared to life, purring loudly in the quiet garage. It took me a few seconds to locate the garage door opener on the dash. I released a grateful breath when the door began rising. Eliza watched me with dark eyes, not saying anything as we pulled carefully out of the garage into an evening shower.

The gate to Willoughby Place's private drive was open. Was I supposed to see it as a sign of good faith? I was being allowed to leave. How big of Tod Belmond and his posse. Still, I wasn't going to squander my good fortune. The farther I got from him and his lies, the better. Not that I had any idea where to go. Rain lashed the windshield as I slowly drove the streets of Hampstead. I didn't know London. I'd been driven during most of my time here, and even if I did have a handle on the city, I didn't belong anywhere. I hadn't cried since I left the house, but my eyes ached from earlier and my skin was tight where my tears had fallen.

"Should we go back to Bexby?" I asked Eliza.

"Do you want to?" she asked carefully. "Maybe we should just pull over and talk."

That was actually a great idea. Maneuvering my car to the side of the street, I put it in park and stared ahead. Darkness chased the twilight, autumn already cutting the days short. Time was running out, and I didn't know what to do.

Eliza didn't say anything as we sat there. When I couldn't take the silence any longer, I searched for something to say that would cut through the tension that had formed since our hasty departure. But there was only one thing I kept coming back to.

"Do you think I'm crazy?" I blurted out.

"I'm not sure how to answer that," she admitted. I threw a scorching look at her and she continued on quickly, "I mean, I think this situation is mental, and you are part of this situation. So..."

That was a yes if I ever heard one.

I sighed, closing my eyes, and thought of a better question. "Do you believe them?"

"I don't know them," she said firmly. "But you do, so I guess what matters is do you believe them?"

I wanted to shake my head, but it wouldn't move. I swallowed as I found myself unable to speak.

"It's okay," Eliza said softly. She tilted her head to meet my eyes. "Hey, can I smoke in this bitch's car?"

I couldn't help laughing as I nodded. "Go ahead."

I appreciated that she hadn't lumped me in with Kerrigan. She hadn't said *your* car. It didn't mean she believed me, but it made me feel like I was still Kate to her.

Eliza rolled the window down just enough that rain wouldn't get in and lit her cigarette. She held out the opened pack. I started to decline, changed my mind, and took one. If there was ever a night to do something out of character, this would be it. But I didn't light it.

"You want me to burn their house down?" she asked.

My head swiveled to stare at her.

"What?" She shrugged. "I've got your back. You say burn it down, I've already got the lighter."

"I don't think that will be necessary, but I appreciate the offer," I said. I had no desire to inspire arson, but it was comforting to know that Eliza was behind me no matter what. "I just don't understand what's going on."

"That makes two of us." She blew a stream of smoke toward the cracked window. "I mean, it would explain the shitty waitressing."

I laughed humorlessly. It would, but it wouldn't explain much else—like my whole life until this moment.

"I mean, why would he lie?" she asked me.

"Marrying his daughter into the Byrd family is all he cares about," I told her. "He basically groomed Kerrigan to be the ideal wife for Spencer since she was little. He wants the family title."

"But if he's lying and you aren't...why would he want a stranger to marry Spencer?"

"It will still be her name," I said miserably.

"And if she comes back?" Eliza pressed. "Where does he expect you to go?"

"I think that's where the ten million pounds comes in." I'd known it was an insane amount of money when he first dangled the offer in front of me. I had expected it to come with strings, but I was quickly discovering most of them weren't visible to me at the time. I thought giving up my virginity was the biggest sacrifice I'd be asked to make. It felt like nothing now.

"Well, he's stupid then." Eliza's directness caught me off-guard. "A story like this: orphan paid to masquerade as an heiress and marry the future Prime

Minister? That story will be worth a lot more than ten million."

She had a point. The realization settled over me with a dull numbness that felt terribly like dread. Tod Belmond must have known that in London's gossip-hungry culture, I could get that much or more just for inside information.

"Think about it, K. You could sell book rights, movie rights, go on talk shows," she continued. "You could make a fortune."

Her words twisted inside me until it felt like I couldn't breathe.

"It's impossible," I whispered. "I'm not Kerrigan Belmond."

Eliza nodded, tossing her cigarette butt out the window. "If that's what—"

"Where did we meet?" I cut her off before she could cast her lot in with mine.

"At the pub." She studied me for a minute. "Don't you remember?"

"It's just a little fuzzy."

"You came in asking about flats to rent," she prompted.

"That's right." I had found myself in Bexby with nowhere to stay and no money. I'd asked about flats and then I'd asked about jobs. "You said you needed a flatmate."

"I did."

"You barely knew me." A terrible thought occurred to me.

"There are like five people living in West Bexby. I didn't have a lot of options. Besides, you seemed nice, and I was pretty sure I could take you in a fight if you came at me with a butcher knife."

She had a point there, but it was a lot to swallow when I looked back. "Tod had pictures of me at our flat and at the pub. He knew I was there before he came to talk to me."

"He was spying on us," Eliza shrieked.

She was either really committed to her part or this was all news to her. I was too exhausted by today's events to try to decide which. "Did you know? Did he come to you?"

"To me?" She took out another cigarette, shaking her head with an indignant grunt. "I can see why you'd ask me, but nope. I didn't, but there is something I need to tell you."

The weight that had begun to lift off my chest slammed down again.

"A couple of months back, I started finding these envelopes under our door."

My mouth went dry. "What was inside them?"

"A couple of hundred quid," she confessed.

"From who?"

"I don't know." She lit up again and took a long drag off her cigarette.

"And you didn't tell me? What did you do with it?"

"I paid the rent and bought food and paid the elec-tric," she shot back defensively. "Where I'm from you don't ignore free money, and I didn't tell you because I knew you would be all weird about it."

"Because it was weird, Eliza." I slumped down in the seat. "It had to be from Tod."

"Maybe." Eliza wiggled next to me before groan-ing. "K, I'm sorry. I shouldn't have done that without telling you, but please, believe me, I didn't know about any of this."

I looked into the night ahead. Lights had begun to appear in the blackness. It was impossible given the storm to discern if they were stars or houses or cars. In the dark, it didn't matter. Light was light.

I was in the dark. I had no idea which direction to go. Trusting Eliza might be a mistake, but she was the first light to shine in my night. I had to choose between continuing into the unknown or choosing to follow that light.

"I'm not mad," I said finally. "I'm just confused."

"I don't blame you." She knocked her shoulder into mine. "But hey, what if you are an heiress? I think you should buy me two diamond tiaras."

"And where are you going to wear all these tiaras?" I asked dryly. I didn't know how she managed to keep her sense of humor, but it was a relief one of us could.

"At the pub," she teased. "I'll get so many tips."

I could only imagine Eliza serving fish and chips in

a crown in West Bexby. It would be the talk of the town.

"How do I find out?" I asked her.

"DNA test?"

I nodded. That made sense, but it also took time. "And until then I just sit and obsess over it." And continue to fill Kerrigan's shoes.

"I'm not sure you have much of a choice unless..."

"I'm open to suggestions."

"Is there anyone you trust? Someone who wouldn't lie to you?"

I swallowed at the nervous ache her words prompted in my chest. There was one person who had to know the truth. I hit the ignition switch and swerved onto the road. "Where are you staying?"

"My aunt's," Eliza answered.

"Look, I have something to take care of. Can I drop you off at her house?"

"Just take me to the nearest tube station," Eliza suggested. I started to protest but she held up a hand to stop me. "You have enough on your plate. But I am curious. Where are we going?"

"To see a friend."

CHAPTER THREE

Friend was a loose term, I realized as I pulled past the gate of Sparrow Court nearly a half-hour later. I felt terrible for ditching Eliza, but somehow I knew it would be worse to drag her farther into this mess. I couldn't imagine what she thought of me or any of us, for that matter. My stomach did a flip-flop when I spotted Spencer's McLaren and Holden's SUV parked in the front-drive. Both of them were here, but I only came to see one of them. Part of me wanted to turn around and keep driving until I was out of London. Kerrigan ran for a reason. Shouldn't I see that as a warning?

But if there was any truth to Tod's claims, I needed to know.

I dashed through the rain to the front door and knocked. I expected a butler to answer, but instead, Evie opened the door. She wore a tired frown, but she mustered up a smile when she saw me. It was missing her customary dimples. That wasn't surprising given her grandfather's sudden death. Even though Lord Byrd had been fairly terrible to his grandchildren, it had to be hard. Regrets often accompany grief as much as sadness. Something told me that the Byrds had a lot of regrets.

Without a thought, I stepped forward and wrapped my arms around her. I was here for answers, but I couldn't ignore her pain. Evie hugged me back awkwardly as if she was out or practice with open displays of affection.

"How are you?" I asked.

"Superfluous," she said flatly. "I'm just trying to stay out of everyone's way. Mother hasn't stopped drinking. I think it's her new profession. Spencer's been in with the family lawyers for hours. I'm sure he'll be glad for the interruption."

"Actually." I bit my lower lip, gathering the courage to plunge forward. "I need to talk to Holden."

Evie's head tilted and she studied me for a moment with a puzzled expression. "I think he's in the Billiards room. I'll show you."

Of course, he was. His grandfather had just died. Why wouldn't he be enjoying himself? I wondered briefly if he'd tried to be supportive or if he'd just found a quiet place to hide. Evie filled me in on the details of what had happened while we walked. After Spencer had returned to me in Yorkshire, their grandfather had seemed completely fine. But when he didn't show for his morning breakfast, a maid found him in his room. He had died peacefully in his sleep. Given how he'd treated his family in life, it felt like too good an ending for him. I kept that thought to myself, but I heard the relief in Evie's voice as she told me.

I wondered how Spencer felt. I wondered how Holden felt.

"Holden comes here when he's avoiding the family," she explained as she led me to a heavy oak door. "If I had to guess where he disappeared to..."

The crack of balls bouncing from an opening shot was the first clue we were on the right track. We paused outside the door, and I took a deep breath.

"Do you mind if I have a minute with him?" I asked.

Evie's face fell, and I felt terrible. She'd been dismissed by the rest of the family. Now I was doing the same thing to her. "I'll just be a minute," I promised her. "Then maybe we can go grab a bite to eat."

"That's okay. I think I'm going to bed." She forced a polite smile and gave me a hug goodbye. This one was slightly less awkward than the first. I made a mental note that Evie might need to experience affection on her own terms. But in truth, I was relieved that she didn't want to hang out. Still, if everyone else was going to ignore her, I would have pushed all this drama aside to see she wasn't alone. Despite her brave face, her shoulders slumped as she started down the hall.

She got a few steps before she turned. "Is everything okay with you and Spencer?"

"Yes," I said a bit too quickly, my hand already reaching toward the door. "Everything's fine. Why?"

Her eyes strayed to the door to the Billiards Room. "I just...be careful, Kerrigan."

"I will," I promised, wondering if others had picked up on the tension between me and Holden. Spencer had, but my fake fiancé had fanned the flames of that tension intentionally. Did Evie see it as well? Part of me worried that I was about to make things worse. Evie's warning lingered in my mind as I knocked softly on the door. I didn't wait for a response before I opened it and stepped inside.

A half-empty bottle of Scotch sat on the edge of the pool table, no glass in sight. Holden looked up for a moment before returning to his shot. His cue slid confidently between his fingers and sent the six ball into the back pocket. He dropped the pool cue on the table and reached for the bottle. Taking a big swig, he held it out to me. I guessed that explained the lack of glasses.

I shook my head. "I'm driving."

His eyes narrowed at my words and I regretted telling him. In the dim lighting, there was no hint of blue in his dark gaze. "I thought I told you not to do that."

Something inside snapped. "This may come as a surprise, but I don't do what you tell me."

I'd made the mistake of admitting that I had panic

attacks to Holden along with revealing a few more choice secrets. He'd been pissed with me for driving in Yorkshire after one of my attacks.

He snorted as he abandoned the bottle and picked his cue back up. "Tell me about it. You never have."

"What does that mean?" I demanded. It wasn't the first time he'd dropped a cryptic comment. I'd tried to ignore them before because I thought he was trying to rile me up. Now I wondered if there was more to these comments than I'd previously thought.

"Nothing," he muttered. "Come to soothe poor Spencer's sorrow?"

Of course, that's why he thought I was here. It was the most reasonable explanation, after all. Hadn't I offered to be by Spencer's side earlier? Wasn't that my place? It was clear Holden believed that as much as he resented it.

"I came to see you," I admitted.

Holden paused, his body poised over the table. Then took his shot. The ball clipped the edge of the pocket and rolled across the table.

"Fuck," he said with a grunt. "Well, dirty girl, if we aren't drinking, what did you come for?"

I swallowed. He wasn't going to make this easy. I'd expected that, but now that I was here, I wasn't certain I could ask him about Tod's claims. But why? Holden had the power to dismiss Tod's lies outright. He could prove that Tod was ruthlessly acting in his own interest. He could set me free. More importantly, he could assure me that I wasn't crazy.

"It's about Kerrigan," I began. Suddenly, I didn't know where to start.

Holden arched an eyebrow. "What about her?"

"It's just..." I searched for the right words. He already knew about the arrangement. This should be easy, but it was anything but. "I found some of her things in Tod's office a few weeks ago and then tonight, I found a file, and he wants me to see a doctor, and I'm not crazy, but—"

"Whoa, slow down," Holden stopped me. "You're going a little fast."

"Sorry." I sighed and walked over to a club chair in the corner. I sank into its rich brown leather, my fingers clutching its arms. "So much has happened."

"Go back to his office. You said you found something?"

"Yes, Kerrigan's computer."

Holden fell silent, remaining in the shadows. The moment stretched between us for so long that I opened my mouth to ask him what was wrong. Before I could, he crossed to the chair next to mine and took it.

"What else?" he asked gently.

"A folder." My voice trembled, and he reached a handout. Placing it on my knee, he waited. "There were photos and bank statements. He's been tracking Kerrigan. I just don't understand why."

Holden remained quiet, and I found myself unable

to bear it.

"And there were pictures of me. He'd found me somehow and had me followed."

"Why would he do that?" Darkness coated his words, and I looked up to find him watching me carefully.

"Because he thinks I'm her."

I didn't know what to expect when I told Holden this, but I'd hoped it would provide some clue as to the truth. But he didn't react. He sat there, his hand warm on my knee and his face a blank mask.

"Holden," my voice broke on his name. "He lied to me. He doesn't want me to pretend to be her. He's going to force me to..."

"To what?" Holden pressed. "What do you think he's planning?"

Before I'd walked into Sparrow Court, I was certain that this was part of some desperate scheme on Tod Belmond's part to ensure what he wanted most: the marriage of his daughter to Spencer Byrd.

"He's obsessed with uniting his family with yours. I don't think he cares if it's me or Kerrigan marrying Spencer."

Holden's eyes closed briefly, a grimace of pain contorting his face.

"I know you don't want her to marry him," I added quietly.

He looked up at me and shook his head. "You still don't get it, dirty girl. I don't want *you* to marry him."

CHAPTER FOUR

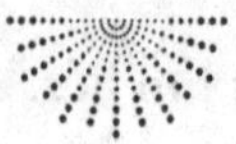

"Because then he wins?" I don't know why I thought Holden could see past his rivalry with Spencer long enough to care about Tod's treachery.

"Is that what you think this is about?" Holden asked darkly.

"Why would I think anything else? First, you loved Kerrigan. Then you wanted me. Your affection doesn't last longer than the next distraction," I exploded. Jumping to my feet, I turned to go. "I don't know why I came here. I'm sorry for interrupting your grieving process."

Holden's hand shot out and caught my arm before I could leave. I tugged half-heartedly at his grip but couldn't find the strength to pull away. I'd come here for answers, but I was going to leave more confused than ever.

"Why did you come to me?" he asked roughly.

"Believe me, I'm asking myself the same question," I spit back. I didn't have an answer. Why had I believed Holden held the key to the secrets I needed to unlock?

"Try again," he said in a soft voice. "Why did you come to me?"

I stilled and stared at him, waiting for him to explain what he meant. When he didn't, I felt the last of my patience dissolve. "I don't know," I snapped. "I thought you would tell me the truth."

"Is that what you're after?" He studied me for a moment. His pupils were dilated from the low light and alcohol. I smelled its warmth on his breath, almost as hot as the hand wrapped around my wrist.

"What else would I be here for?" I asked, but my own mouth went dry as soon as the question left my mouth. There was another reason I was here. With him so close to me, it was impossible to ignore that fact. I'd come looking for both answers and comfort. I had been so sure that Holden could offer me both. "I'm sorry I came."

I tried to pull away, but he merely shifted and drew me into his arms. An ache filled me as our bodies crashed softly together. Holden made no move to touch me even though I was close enough to kiss. Instead, his arms wrapped around me, cradling me close to his hard body. This was wrong. I wasn't supposed to be here with him. He wasn't the one that I should have come to, but even as my thoughts waged war in my head, a peacefulness settled in my chest. It only lasted a fraction of a second before I pushed it away along with Holden. I stumbled back a few steps and shook my head.

"I can't do this," I murmured.

His head dropped, his shoulders following, and he didn't respond. Finally, he drew a long breath and lifted his head. "What?"

"This," I whispered. "Us."

His eyes closed as his hands balled into fists. When he finally opened them, hollow pain looked back at me. "Which one of you?"

"What?" I shook my head, trying to clear the lingering effects of his presence.

"Which one of you can't do this?" he asked, his tone rich with pain.

"I'm tired of the riddles," I said. Anger surged through me like the billowing clouds of a fast-approaching storm. "Just say what you mean."

"I don't think I have to, dirty girl," he said sadly. "I think you just have to listen."

I thought of the last time I'd seen him in Yorkshire and what he'd said. "Why did you say Kerrigan isn't coming back?"

He knew something. Was it the same thing Tod had found out? Is that why all of this was happening?

"She's gone." His lips turned up in a half-smile that stole my breath. "I'm not sure she was ever really here."

"I can't just replace her." The words pitched out of me with a slight shriek. "I won't."

I waited for him to speak, clinging to the hope like a life preserver in a storm. He had to help me. Holden could find her. He cared about me. He wouldn't let me marry Spencer in her place. I knew why he didn't want me to marry him. I was sure of it, so why was he playing games with me?

"Why not?" he pushed. "You seem happy with Spencer. You'll want for nothing."

"How can you say that?" I asked breathlessly. "You of all people?"

"What?" he roared. "What about me? Why am I important? Tell me, Kerrigan!"

"How can you give up?" The question I'd tried to keep inside me tore from my mouth, ripping my heart out along with it. "Why won't you fight for me?"

Then, I realized what he'd done. He called me Kerrigan. I caught my breath and held it, waiting for him to respond. He stared at me for a minute before his face contorted into a mirthless grin.

"I've never stopped fighting for you," he said with a hollow laugh. "I waited. I listened. I loved you more than I've ever loved another soul, including my own—and you left me for her. And when you came back..."

"*Her*?" I blinked in confusion and was surprised when tears fell from my lashes. I hadn't realized I was crying.

"Kate," he said the name with spite. "*Her*. I

thought it was a twisted joke, and then I realized it was so much worse than that."

Holden was drunk. He wasn't making sense. It had been foolish to come to him, but even stupider to stay after I smelled the Scotch on his breath. Did he even know he was talking to me? Did he think I was her?

"How much have you had to drink?" I pointed to the bottle.

"I opened that one for the occasion," he informed me. "We're celebrating around here. The old tyrant is dead, but that doesn't change the truth about you, dirty girl."

"You're drunk. I should go." I turned to walk away.

"Just face it already," he yelled. "Stop pretending!"

"What are you saying, Holden?" I asked slowly because I wasn't certain I wanted to know the answer.

"You know what I'm saying." He moved toward me, closing the distance between us. His fingers gripped my chin as he brought my gaze level with his own. Answers burned in his irises, and, as much as I wanted to, I couldn't turn away. "I loved you from the first moment we met. I hated you just as long because I always knew you weren't mine. I knew you could never be mine. And when you ran, I stupidly thought you'd chosen me. I looked for you. I found you before Tod. I made sure you had money, and I waited for you to realize you were safe—that you could stop pretending. But you never stopped. You're still doing it."

At some point, I'd started to sob, but Holden didn't

stop. His eyes burned into mine, burrowing past the stories and confusion and lies into my soul itself.

"And the worst part is, that even as her, you chose him," he said flatly.

Words I didn't quite understand found themselves on my lips. "I didn't have a choice. Spencer was part of the arrangement."

He laughed again, and the cold hatred in it chilled me to the bone. "You still think this is about Spencer? After everything, Kerrigan?"

"Don't call me Kerrigan," I said, half-whisper, half plea.

"*Kerrigan*," he repeated. "Who is this really about?"

I closed my eyes and shook my head. "I'm not..."

The refusal died on my lips. I couldn't find the words to fight it any longer.

He released my chin, but I didn't open my eyes. Holden trailed the back of his hand down my cheek. "It's going to be okay. I promise."

"Why would I believe you?" I asked with a swallow.

"Because I love you."

But I was already pulling away. His words didn't matter. He'd betrayed me. He'd lied to me. He'd manipulated me and played Spencer's games. He was worse than Tod. He was worse than all of them. He would blind himself to have her back. I couldn't trust him. Not when he couldn't see straight. But when I looked at him, I found the last thing I ever expected to see written across his handsome face.

Hope.

Anger swelled inside me until it boiled over, bursting from me. How could he look at me like that? How could he dare to love me after this? He hated me? I hated him more. It burned inside me in a molten rage, and I turned and released it with devastating force. "Then you're either stupid or blind because I could never trust you. And if I can't trust you, then I will never love you."

His mouth fell open slightly and he stared back at me. Holden's eyebrows raised in disbelief before he found a bemused smile. It was as empty as his eyes.

"What the fuck do you think is funny about this?" I seethed.

"I withdraw my previous statement," he said flatly. "I was wrong. You aren't gone."

I opened my mouth to interrupt him, but it was too late. The words were already free of his mouth.

"Welcome back, Kerrigan."

CHAPTER FIVE

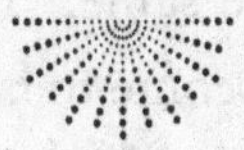

Holden didn't follow me as I flew out the door—away from him and his lies. I was a few steps from leaving Sparrow Court behind me, hopefully forever, when Spencer opened the door to his grandfather's study. He paused, surprise flashing across his handsome face when he found me rushing past him.

"Kerrigan," he called, but I continued.

I couldn't stop. I needed to break free before I found my cage locked forever. Behind me, heavy footsteps followed me quickly. I'd nearly reached the front door when a palm slammed into the wood panel, preventing me from opening it.

"Where are you going? I was calling you!" Spencer sounded tired, and I looked up to see exhaustion written over his face. But it wasn't from lack of sleep. This was exhaustion that only came from carrying the heavier burdens of life. It was a weight Spencer had carried since his father died. It had been there since the moment we met, but tonight it looked heavier than normal. Now that another death marked his life, I wondered how it would weigh him down. I wondered if he would ever be the same. "Evie told me you were here. She said I should come to find you."

A jolt of betrayal blasted through me. "Evie shouldn't have done that." I hoped he didn't catch how my voice trembled with anger. "I just came by to give something to Holden. I found it in my things from Yorkshire."

Spencer shifted his body and slumped against the door. He did a good job of looking like he was simply relaxing, but I couldn't shake the feeling that he was bracing it against my departure. It was as if he was trapping me himself. "What was that?"

"Huh?" I asked, feeling confused.

"What did you give him?" Ice crackled in his words. He already suspected Holden had feelings for me. Now I realized that he suspected I shared those feelings.

I gave him a piece of my mind. But I couldn't say that out loud. Not without having an explanation, and, the truth was that Spencer wasn't entirely wrong in his suspicions. "A notebook. I borrowed it at Haworth."

"With all the chaos, I forgot you went there with him," Spencer said bitterly. "If I had known all of this would happen...I should have stayed in Yorkshire with you."

Despite the confusion, I felt about Spencer and his family, pity took hold of me. "But at least you got to say goodbye to your grandfather," I pointed out. "If you hadn't returned, you wouldn't have seen him one last time."

"Do you think I care about that?" A cruel, unfamiliar laugh spilled from him. "I would rather have been with you. We could have done much more interesting things than visit the homes of old, dead women."

I'd already told Spencer that I enjoyed the moors and the Brontës' home. He hadn't heard me then. He wouldn't hear me now. I seemed to only matter within the context of his own existence.

"Maybe next time," I said flatly, knowing there would be no next time. Not for us.

"Something's different about you," Spencer said in a quiet tone. His green eyes studied me intently. I wondered if he could see the truth. Could he tell that I was lying? Could he see that I knew something? Did he know something himself?

But I wasn't the only one that had changed. Everything was different since Yorkshire. The world had shifted on its axis and now things felt upside down and inside out. It was as though I was looking in a mirror. Holden loved me. Spencer coveted me. I was Kerrigan, not Kate. I belonged to this world, not the one I left behind. None of it made any sense, and the longer I stayed here trying to understand, the crazier I felt.

"I need to go. I have a headache," I lied. It was a lame excuse, but Spencer's face softened, the cruel manipulativeness vanishing. Concern replaced it. How did he change direction so easily? Was it the gift of a politician or something else entirely?

I'd once thought that Holden was the unreadable brother. I was beginning to wonder if Spencer was hiding even more secrets.

"A headache? You should say then," Spencer said.

"Don't be silly. You have your hands full. I'll see you tomorrow." I kept my eyes on the door, not trusting myself to look at him. I reached for the doorknob, but he caught my wrist.

"Why don't you tell me the truth?" The question seethed from him.

I pulled away, trying to break free of his grip, but his fingers tightened. "Let go. You're hurting me."

He ignored me. "Is something going on between you and Holden?"

I laughed, not because it was a ludicrous accusation. But because his timing was highly suspect. Despite having the weight of his family's legacy on his shoulders, Spencer cared more about whether a woman he barely knew, who was the subject of an arranged marriage, wanted someone else. "No," I said, frustration growing hot tendrils in my chest. "I hate Holden."

"That's what I was afraid of," Spencer said darkly. For a moment, he looked so much like his twin that I shrunk under his gaze. "What does that mean?"

"I think you know exactly what it means," he said, his voice dropping to an accusatory whisper. I waited for him to explain what he meant. Instead, he continued his interrogation. "Did you fuck him in Yorkshire?"

"What?" I sputtered. "Did I what?"

"Did you fuck him?" he repeated, each word popped out of his lips with hateful force.

"No." I yanked my hand free, barely resisting the urge to slap him.

His head hung for a moment, a gesture I mistook for shame, until he asked his next question, "Did you want to?"

The words pierced me and struck me momentarily silent.

"I see," he said, a muscle ticking his jaw. "I guess that's my answer."

I shook my head. He didn't see. He didn't understand. Spencer had no idea what was going on, but that wouldn't stop him from making judgments. He thought I wanted to sleep with his brother. Maybe he was right. In fact, I knew he was, even if that desire had lulled. I had asked Holden to take me to bed. But he didn't know me. Kate asked Holden to go to bed, not Kerrigan. Spencer had no claim to the real me nor did he know what was at stake. He had no idea how deeply we were all mired in lies. And it didn't matter, because there was a fundamental flaw in our relationship.

Spencer Byrd believed he owned me.

I had a lot of questions, but I knew one thing for certain. No one owned me.

"Since you're so interested in Holden's dick," I began, "why don't you go fuck him yourself?"

His mouth fell open, and I took advantage of his stunned silence, to throw open the door and bolt toward the safety of London.

CHAPTER SIX

There was nowhere for me to go. I couldn't return to Willoughby Place, where Tod waited to lure me into his trap. It wasn't as if I could go and lock myself in Kerrigan's room. For all I knew, they had cameras on it, spying on me the whole time. I wouldn't stay with Spencer, even if I had a key to his flat. There was too great a possibility that he or Holden might show up. Although, given Holden's condition, I hoped he wouldn't drive. I considered calling Eliza, but I couldn't stomach the thought of reliving tonight if only to catch her up on what had happened.

But most of all, I wanted to be alone. The kind of alone where there would be no casual conversation or accidental interactions. Solitude like that wasn't easy to find in London.

I needed to be anonymous, so I drove. In a city as

big as London, it was easy to get lost. I found myself driving beyond the limits of Hampstead into its busy streets, searching for the solitude of crowds. Maneuvering the roads was easier than it should be, and doubt took hold at the back of my mind. Holden claimed I was Kerrigan. Tod claimed I was Kerrigan. Iris. Giles. Why would they all lie?

That was why I couldn't go back to her world. I couldn't face the idea that I was trapped in it for the rest of my life. Only days ago, I'd wondered how I could leave Kerrigan behind. Then, I had thought I was in love with Spencer. Now? I wasn't sure of anything.

Outside the windscreen, it began to drizzle, raindrops splattering the glass until I had to turn on the wiper blades. The rain, coupled with nightfall, slowly cleared the streets. A few strangers straggled down the sidewalks while others dashed toward well-lit buildings. I found myself jealous of them, wishing I had someplace to go. A place that didn't require me to rush like those taking their time on the sidewalks. Or a place where I could run in from the rain without worry. Instead, I was stuck in limbo, torn between heaven and hell. I had no choice but to continue.

Before long, I found myself driving near the Thames. The London Eye spun slowly in the background, a slave to tourists if not the weather. Near it, the clock tower was lit up like a beacon of all that London represented. I thought of the first time I saw it.

Or was it just the most recent time? I'd been here with Spencer, checking into the Westminster Royal. London's beacon had done its job and pointed me in a direction, at last. The hotel was well-lit and safe and welcoming for a price. I'd forgotten for a moment that anything could be bought, even a place to go. I pulled to the side of the road and found its address on my mobile. I was only a few minutes from it. At least, it was familiar. At best, it was anonymous.

I steered the Porsche up to the valet stand near its front entrance. A parking attendant met me at the entrance, perching a long-handled umbrella over my door as he opened it.

"Do you have any bags, miss?"

I shook my head, my fingers tightening over the Chanel clutch Giles had given me. "No. I'm here to meet someone."

I wasn't sure why I lied. Maybe because it was odd to show up at a hotel without a suitcase. Maybe because I didn't want one more person to look at me like I'd lost my mind tonight.

"Would you like me to park the car in overnight parking?"

I nodded before I realized what a woman showing up to meet someone at a hotel insinuated. Heat blossomed on my cheeks, but I lifted my head higher. It's not as if I were the first woman to meet a man at the hotel if that was why I'd come here. But it wasn't as if that was why I was here. So why did it matter, at all?

But as I walked into the polished lobby of the five-star hotel, I wished I was more dressed for the occasion. Without the armor of the Porsche, I was just a woman with no makeup and a messy bun in jeans and sneakers.

Why does that matter? I asked myself. I'd come to London months ago wearing secondhand clothes without a cent to my name. Now the jeans I wore were designer, I held a Chanel clutch in my hand, and the name Kerrigan Belmond was on my identification and credit cards. For all intents and purposes, I belonged here. Wasn't that what everyone was trying to prove to me?

So why did I feel like a fraud?

I made my way across the lobby to the registration desk, cringing as my sneakers squeaked on the marble floors. The girl at registration whipped her head up at the sound, but she smiled when she saw me. "Checking in?"

"I hope so," I said, feeling a little nervous. Spencer had dropped his name the night we showed up here without a reservation and the world had rearranged itself in his presence. That was the way it was for people with money. But no matter what my identification said or who people believed me to be, it made me uncomfortable to act so demandingly. "I don't have a reservation. I just need a room for the night."

"Let me see what I can do." Her attitude remained gracious, which meant I didn't look as thrown together as I felt, or she was genuinely kind. Her own dark hair was pulled into a smart knot at the back of her neck and her plum lipstick brightened her ready smile when she said, "I have a single room available if that's okay?"

The last time I stayed at the Westminster Royal, I'd been in a private suite that took up an entire floor of the hotel. Spencer had demanded it, as though two people needed more than a bed and a roof over their heads. I didn't require that much space. In fact, I didn't want it. "That would be perfect."

She took my identification and credit card, chattering away in a friendly manner as she filled me in on the hotel's amenities. It wasn't until she began typing the information from my identification that she stopped mid-sentence. "I apologize, Ms. Belmond. I see that you are a platinum elite member of the Eaton family of hotels. Let me see about getting you an upgrade."

"That won't be necessary," I said quickly. I should have known something like this was inevitable, whether or not I name dropped. "I'm simply grateful that you can get me a room on such short notice."

"Are you sure?" She chewed on her lips thoughtfully, watching me like she was taking a test.

"I travel a lot," I lied. I'd never gone anywhere. Kerrigan had. "That's the reason I have that platinum status."

"Standard procedure is to offer an upgrade in such

cases," she explained. "I'm sure we can find you a nicer room —"

"A single is fine," I repeated firmly. "I just need a place to sleep."

She continued after another minute of hesitation. She prepped a key card and passed it to me in a little envelope. Her friendliness seemed to have cooled. She was on edge as though she knew the name Kerrigan Belmond came with more than just an elite status. I took the key with one last hopeful smile. The one she mustered looked more concerned than cordial.

That was one of the worst parts of being Kerrigan: the expectation that came with her name. Maybe she lived up to the stereotype of the overprivileged heiress. Maybe no one ever gave her a chance to prove she was anything else. I considered it as I took the lift up a floor and continued down a corridor toward my room.

When I found it, I unlocked it to discover a room about the size of the presidential suite's closet. The door opened to a double bed, with two nightstands crammed into the corners beside it, and just enough space to walk its perimeter. The attached bathroom had a simple, cramped shower stall, toilet, and sink. Everything was neatly appointed and sparkling clean, but it was a far cry from the luxurious space I knew was sitting on the top floor. There was a time when a hotel room this nice would have been entirely outside my means. I'd only recently found myself in that luxurious, overindulgent suite.

Which one did I belong in? The sidewalk outside the hotel as Kate? Or the penthouse meant for people like Kerrigan? I comforted myself that limbo seemed to be somewhere in between in a warm, cozy room with a locked door and a pillow.

I checked both the locks and threw the extra bolt so that no one could get inside the room. Then I walked over to open the drapes. Nighttime in London was different than the quiet, all-consuming dark of Yorkshire. At night, London was alive. Lights dazzled along the streets, cars sped by, and, despite the continued rain, umbrellas once again dotted the sidewalks as the world kept spinning, even in the storm. I lost track of time as I stood and watched the rain hit the windowpanes, its pitter-patter lulling me into a daze. At some point, it began to come down harder, lashing the glass with a mesmerizing force that I found equally captivating. The night seemed to seep into the room and with each second, I became more aware of the cold, wet world around me. I could almost feel the rain on my shoulders. I drop hit my face and instinctively, I looked up to see where it had fallen. But there was nothing there. My interest in the dazzling world outside the window was replaced by an intense study of the ceiling. There was no wet spot and no sign of a leak. That wasn't surprising since I was on the second floor. There was nothing above me but pristine plaster. Beneath me, the floor rocked, and I finally realized that it wasn't the storm I had felt but the familiar tendrils of an anxiety attack. I tried to turn to the bed. I only needed to spin around to reach it, but shifting direction only made it worse. Panic hit me like waves of icy water and my knees buckled.

I didn't try to fight it as I crumbled to the ground. It was said and strong. There was something else. The floor moved again, and I threw myself forward, grabbing hold of the mattress. It tilted as though it were a capsizing boat. I clung to the blankets, but there was no anchor in the storm. It had finally found me, and there was no safe harbor.

"Kerrigan!"

I lifted my head to look for the voice that called my name. I expected to find Spencer standing at the door. But it was still closed and bolted like I'd left it. Blackness shadowed its edges like night was claiming it. Which was real: the darkness or the door? I dropped my head onto the mattress top, my stomach churning from the tumultuous storm. "This isn't real," I whispered to myself.

In the past when the darkness found me, it overtook me. There was no such relief tonight. It battered me from all sides until I was sobbing and soaked in sweat. I kept hearing my name called, but I didn't dare look up. I knew I had locked up, meaning it was impossible for someone else to be in here with me. But the name hung in the air like an echo. Was it a trick of my mind? Or something much darker? I stayed at the edge of the bed until calm descended. When I was certain that everything was fine, I finally lifted my head and opened my eyes.

I was alone in a hotel room on the second floor of the Westminster Royal. There was no rain seeping through the ceiling. No violent waves rocking the floor. No person at the door calling my name. Despite that, my fingers remained tightly on the sheets until I pried them free. I didn't dare stand up. Instead, I placed one shaky palm to the floor and lowered myself to my hands and knees. The dizzying effects of the attack lingered, even as I made my way slowly to the bathroom, speeding up as my mouth began to water. Thankfully, I reached the toilet before I vomited. Collapsing onto the tile beneath me, I lay shaking until I found the strength to draw my mobile from my pocket and dial a number.

The phone picked up on the first ring. I didn't wait for him to answer.

"I'm at the Westminster Royal. I need you." Then, I hung up.

CHAPTER SEVEN

By the time I heard the knock at the door, I'd managed to pull myself up off the floor. I turned the handle, sagging against the wall for support, and opened the door to find him standing there. I hated the relief I felt as I drank in his broad shoulders and muscular form. He was turned away from me, his hands shoved in his pockets, and as he turned to face me, he wore an expression of confusion.

No, not confusion. Distaste bordering on disdain. "Did they put you in this room?"

It was only then that I noticed his pressed shirt. Even unbuttoned with his tie hanging loosely around his neck, he held himself importantly. His face was clean-shaven and his eyes clear. He hadn't been drinking. The man standing before me hadn't lost control for a second.

Spencer.

I called Holden, but Spencer came. My heart crashed to the floor at our feet, but I mustered a nonchalant look.

"I only asked for a room. I didn't care which one they put me in," I explained.

"When they saw your name, they should've known better than to put you in this." He peered over my shoulder and looked at the room like he'd found me sitting in a hovel.

"It's fine," I said, knowing that he wouldn't listen. "What are you doing here?"

"Evie told me that you called." His eyes shifted to study my face, and I wondered if the sadness reflecting back at me was because he'd found me through a messenger or grief over his grandfather's death. I wasn't about to ask him.

I had not called Evie, though. Of course, Holden wouldn't come. He couldn't have been bothered to tell Spencer I'd called. And if he had, it would only add fuel to Spencer's paranoia that something was going on between me and his twin. Betrayal stung my already fraying nerves. I guess I know where I stood with Holden.

"I apologize for earlier," Spencer continued softly. "I shouldn't have spoken to you like that. Of course, you didn't think you could call me. I wish you didn't feel that way, but I understand. I just hope in the future you feel comfortable coming to me directly. Is that too much to ask?"

He spoke so genuinely that I almost believed him. But which was the real Spencer? The cruel one who spoke ugly words in the heat of the moment or the apologetic, thoughtful one standing before me now? A few months ago, I would have let him in, believing him to be the man standing on my doorstep. Now, I wasn't so sure.

"You have your hands full," I said, pressing a finger to my temple. "And I'm not feeling well. Maybe we should talk about this later."

"Nothing is more important to you," he said, taking a step closer. My body reacted to his nearness, and he took advantage, pressing forward until there was no space left between us. "Arrangements can wait until tomorrow. You can't."

We stood and stared at each other, neither of us wanting to give. Even with the dizzying proximity of his body, I knew the last thing I should do was let him walk into that room. Spencer must have sensed that because he continued to insinuate himself into the hotel room. Each movement was calculated to look unintended, even as he backed me into the space. It also brought him closer to me, making it harder to remember why he should stay in the hall and out of my bed.

"Why are you here?" he asked. "Why didn't you go home?"

"I had a fight with Tod." At least, that much was true.

"I see we're all arguing with our family tonight," he said with a wearied sigh. "Sometimes, you just have to escape them, right?"

I nodded. There was no use explaining to him that I wasn't trying to escape my family. Spencer didn't know about my arrangement with Tod or my real identity. He didn't know how horribly wrong things had gone. He didn't know any of it, and he never need to, as far as I was concerned.

"Can I come in?" He looked over my shoulder, his eyes landing on the bed. Then, he grinned shyly at me with the face of an apologetic puppy. "I was waiting for you to ask, but I was getting the feeling that you might not."

"I was trying to decide if I wanted to ask," I admitted. Maybe I didn't want him here, but I didn't want to be alone either. That's why I'd reached out to Holden. And he'd sent Spencer instead. He left me with two choices: face that quiet hell alone or give in to temptation. I was trapped again. This time in a cage that Holden had chosen for me. It was his choice that drew the linchpin. The message was clear. He didn't want me no matter what he claimed.

I stepped to the side to allow Spencer to enter.

He entered, and I closed the door behind him. We stood in the little space the room allowed; a heavy silence weighed down the air between us.

"Are you sure you don't want a bigger room?"

"It doesn't matter, but it seems like it's important to

you," I said, feeling resigned to meeting his preferences. "I'm sure they have something else available if you're planning to stay."

"That's not it." He raked a hand through his hair, shaking his head with frustration. "I feel like everything I say is wrong."

I didn't respond. It was up to Spencer to explain himself or dig his hole deeper. I wouldn't do it for him.

"Everything is happening so fast," he said. "I know that's not an excuse. Grandfather's death just came out of nowhere."

I refrained from pointing out his grandfather's age or his recent health scare suggested otherwise. But if Spencer thought Lord Byrd's death came out of the blue, then he was living in fantasyland. Not that I could blame him for that.

"I have to take his seat in the peerage," he continued, "and there's paperwork and titles and ceremonies and funerals." The list grew and grew, each addition added more bitterly than the last before he finished with, "and the wedding."

"Don't worry about the wedding," I said softly, hoping it sounded reassuring rather than dismissive. There was no reason for him to worry about the wedding. In three months time, I wouldn't marry Spencer. I knew that deep down. I didn't know how to get out of it yet, but I didn't have any choice. I couldn't live as Kerrigan Belmond for the rest of my life even if what Tod claimed was true. "It's only a formality."

"I know," he said and smiled sadly. "I'm sorry it won't be what you wanted it to be. I suppose it can't be helped."

"What do you mean?"

"Mother has already touched base with Iris. They're handling the details. It's likely that taking my seat in the peerage and the original date for the wedding would conflict." Spencer reached out and took my hands. "I know it won't be what you expected with needing to do it so quickly. I'll make it up to you."

"Quickly?" I repeated as my heart began to pound against my breastbone. Nothing could prepare me for the news he'd come to deliver. I already knew that.

"Three weeks. Maybe two if things can get in order."

CHAPTER EIGHT

"Iris said dresses wouldn't be ready. I imagine the more money we throw at it, the better. At least, mother is accustomed to throwing last-minute soirees." His hands squeezed mine, but I felt nothing but a distant pressure. My brain was too busy trying to process all this information. "But soon we will be married and moving on to the next stage of our lives."

Our lives.

"Shouldn't you be worried about your grandfather?" My mouth was dry and my mind was racing. I had to find a way out. There had to be some reason he couldn't argue with or a way to convince him that there was no need to rush. "We should focus on the funeral and your family."

"You are my family, and it can't wait. It was always part of the plan. I would be married by the time I took my seat in Parliament," he explained.

His sweet words lingered bitterly. "But—"

"None of us expected I needed to marry you this quickly," he continued on, ignoring the interruption. "I'm just so glad that I have you to be at my side."

I didn't say anything. There was nothing to say. No words I uttered would change his mind. I had no choice in the matter. That much was clear. The only thing I could do was run, but how? I'd already asked myself that tonight. Kerrigan ran before, and now I was back here in her place. Something had to change, and I had to be the one to change it. The trouble was that I was running out of time.

"About Holden," Spencer continued. "I'm sorry that I didn't trust you. It's just that I see the way he looks at you."

"I can't control the way he looks at me," I said through gritted teeth. Or the way he feels. I could barely control my own feelings.

"I know that. Another reason for us to get married. Knowing you're mine, knowing you're my wife, that's all I want in the world. Sometimes Holden feels like a threat to that."

"Why?"

"Why wouldn't you prefer him?" Spencer swallowed, his mouth dipping into a frown. "He's fun and wild. There are no expectations. No rushed weddings or family arrangements. You wouldn't have to sacrifice anything to be with him."

"And you think that's what I want?" I needed to

understand where Spencer was coming from, even if I didn't believe a word he said.

"No," he said apprehensively, "I think maybe it's what I want. I wish that it could be that way. I wish we could take our time without pressure. Maybe I'm jealous."

I bit my lip, shocked that he'd finally realized this. "You two need to sort this out."

"We will," he promised.

But I knew they wouldn't, not without time or therapy or probably both. Still, I found myself longing to believe him. If only to escape the harsh reality rushing toward me. If Spencer could work this out, I wouldn't be the target of his paranoid regret. Maybe if he could clear his head, he could see that we didn't have to go through with this.

"I don't deserve you, but I need you."

Spencer's words hung in the air, a strange combination of truth and lies. He didn't deserve me. He didn't need me. And yet he did. I was his only chance at salvation. But I was also his punishment. Maybe he was mine as well.

He dropped my hands and raised his palm to my face. Caressing it down the side of my cheek, he murmured, "You are so beautiful."

I hooked an arm around his neck, staring up into his eyes. It wasn't his words that spurred me forward, it was the pain running through them. His anger and hurt had nothing to do with me. Just like mine had nothing to do with him. But I knew that we needed the same thing. Neither of us could run. Neither of us would. Our destinies had been laid before us and while Spencer's cage might be larger than my own, I could see its bars now all the same. We were both kept creatures. At least, if I joined him in his captivity, I could fly freer than in my own.

"Take me to bed," I whispered.

Spencer closed the final space between us, his lips finding mine with an urgency that told me he felt the same way. His arm circled my waist, crushing my body against his and instinct took over. It didn't feel right, but it felt good—and good was better than numb. Good was better than pain. Good was better than fear and anger and confusion. His mouth claimed me, his tongue forcing open my lips to deepen the kiss. A fire ignited where bodies touched, smoldering through me until it reached my core and blazed to life. My arms hooked over his strong shoulders and he accepted my invitation, lifting me from the ground and carrying me to the bed. We broke free from each other only long enough to tear off our clothes and collide once more. We were flesh on flesh. We were wrong. His kiss was wrong. Each touch robbed a bit more from me. Each taste stole a piece of my soul. But there was so little left of it that I didn't care.

Spencer's mouth moved south, cruising down my neck to my collarbone. "God, you're perfect."

His mouth found my breast, and I reared against

him as a canine grazed my nipple. He nipped harder, sucking it between his teeth possessively. Darkness thickened the air, mirroring the turmoil simmering inside me. I sank my nails into his back, digging into his skin and raking down.

"Fuck," he growled, but he took the violence as an invitation. He reached between my legs and wrenched my thighs open. "You want it rough, dirty girl?"

I hated the way Holden's nickname sounded on Spencer's lips. I especially hated how it sent a hot stab of desire straight to my clit.

"Say it again," I licked my tongue across his lower lip.

"You like that thought, don't you?" he said, his eyes shadowed as he brushed the tip of his cock along my aching entrance. "Dirty girl. It's what you really want, isn't it?"

"I want it rough," I murmured with a groan as his cock swept over my clit. "Maybe that makes me dirty."

"I will give it to you any way you want," he promised, pushing in a fraction of an inch and smiling when I gasped. "As long as you promise me one thing."

At the moment, I would promise him the world for his cock. He'd already taken everything else. "Anything."

"You're mine," he said." "Say it. Say you're my dirty girl."

I stared up at him, knowing that this wasn't about me. It should make me sick, but I didn't feel anything but twisted pleasure. He could make me say whatever he wanted, but I wouldn't belong to him. And when he called me dirty girl, I could pretend he was someone else entirely. It was dirty and wicked and wrong.

And I didn't fucking care.

"I'm yours."

Spencer slammed into me and I arced off the bed, tightening my arms around his neck. My fingers knit through his hair, pulling it. I could be his to use as he pleased, but I would use him, too. Wrapping my legs around his waist, I bucked against him. "Harder."

"Tell me to fuck you," he gritted out as he rocked inside me, slowing his thrusts.

"Fuck me. Hard."

He grabbed hold of my hips and drove deep, each stroke more demanding than the last. There was no love as he fucked me, and that made it better. I dropped my head to his shoulder and bit down, sinking my teeth into the hard muscle. Spencer reared for a second before he pushed me onto the bed, his hand on my stomach, and screwed me like he owned me. A palm pinned me to the mattress as he battered every last one of my defenses. He fucked me until I was nothing but a collection of sensations and pleasure and sweet oblivion. I shattered into pieces beneath him and as my climax tightened around his cock, he released inside me with a primal growl that sent a second orgasm surging through me.

When he finished spilling his seed, he rolled to the

side and collapsed. Part of me liked it better this way. We didn't speak. We didn't touch. We'd both gotten exactly what we wanted from each other.

Spencer broke the perfect moment first.

His arm slid around me, drawing me to him. I didn't resist. What was the point? I'd sold my soul to him and signed the contract with my body.

He wrapped his arms around me, closing me in his cage, and he pressed his lips to my forehead. "Kerrigan, I need you by my side through this."

I didn't know what to say, so I said what I was supposed to. "Of course, Spencer. Whatever you want."

CHAPTER NINE

"**T**his is mental."

I shot a withering look over my shoulder at Eliza. Her dark eyes popped open, her mouth forming a small 'oh' as she realized what she said.

"I'm sorry," she squeaked.

I sighed, pausing with my gloved hands wrist-deep in one of Kerrigan's drawers. "I know. I just don't know what else to do."

"Take some of this jewelry, pawn it, and run?" Eliza suggested.

"If only," I muttered as I continued my search. It wasn't like I couldn't sell half of Kerrigan's jewelry and buy myself a yacht. That wasn't the problem. The problem was that no matter whether I ran or whether I stayed, I needed to know the truth. But finding out the truth was complicated.

"What if you just get some hair from Tod?" she asked. We'd been searching for something of Kerrigan's that might have a speck of her DNA on it all day. Since I'd been using her things for months, that was tricky. We had to find something we knew I'd never touched. Eliza's patience was clearly wearing thin. But I couldn't give up. There had to be something, something buried deep within this mammoth closet that contained a bit of her that I'd yet to see.

"I already thought of that. I want to send three samples," I explained. "Something of hers and something of his and mine. I'm going to cover all my bases. And I'm not asking him for it."

"You would think he would want to prove his side of the story to you." Eliza unsnapped another purse and peered inside it. She groaned in frustration and placed it back on the shelf next to a dozen more.

"Yeah, exactly. If he's involved, how can I know that he hasn't tampered with the results or paid someone off?"

"Good point." She set her shoulders and opened another door. "Don't worry. We're going to find something."

I appreciated her resolution. Almost as much as I appreciated her being here with me. Since the night that I confronted Tod, things had been uncomfortable at the house, to say the least. For the most part, he avoided me as much as I avoided him. That couldn't last much longer. Not with Lord Byrd's funeral in a few hours. I was expected to be at Spencer's side, playing the part of his faithful fiancé.

But it wasn't only Tod avoiding me. Only two days had passed since the night I learned that everyone around me believed I was Kerrigan, thanks to Tod's manipulations. I'd returned home the following morning after spending the night with Spencer at the Westminster Royal and waited for one of them to confront me. Or corner me in an attempt to convince me of the truth. No one did. Were they merely biding their time? Or were they gathering their forces for another onslaught? The avoidance left me uneasy. I hardly wanted to speak to them, but it was nerve-wracking to linger in anticipation of what might happen next.

"I think I have something!" Eliza held up a satchel in triumph. "This isn't it yours, is it?"

I took one look at the Louis Vuitton travel bag and shook my head with a wry smirk. "No, all my couture luggage is Gucci. Seriously? If I owned things like that I wouldn't have been buying scratch cards to make rent money."

"You should be nice to me because this isn't just luggage. There's an entire travel kit inside," she told me.

"Has it been used?" I slammed the drawer I'd been searching shut and rushed over.

"Definitely." Eliza pulled a small zippered bag out and opened it. Inside was a toothbrush, a comb, and a myriad variety of other luxury travel-size toiletries. What fabulous destination had Kerrigan jetted off to with these things in tow? It wasn't like her to leave her bags packed up. In fact, she seemed almost fanatical about keeping things straight and in their place.

"Where did you find it?"

Eliza pointed to the lowest shelf in one of Kerrigan's many closets. "It was shoved way back there and off to the side. There's almost a little cubby back there. She must have forgotten it was there."

Or she had hidden it. I swallowed as I considered why she would do that.

"Is there anything else in here?"

"Not really." Eliza shook her head as she looked into it again. "Oh wait."

She fished something out of the bottom of the bag and held it up.

Blood hammered in my veins as I stared at the hospital bracelet in her hand. One end was cut. Probably from being taken off the bearer's wrist after release. "What's that?"

"A pony?" Eliza teased. "It's a hospital bracelet. It says Kerrigan Belmond. That means we're right. This was her bag."

I plucked the hospital bracelet from her fingers and studied it for a moment. It didn't tell me much. Kerrigan's name and the date of admission. It was from nearly 2 years ago. But why? The name of the hospital was the strangest part.

It didn't sound like a hospital at all.

"Do you know anything about Maison de la paix?"

"Sounds French. Never heard of it," Eliza said. "What's wrong?"

"Nothing," I said quickly. I dropped the bracelet back in the bag and thrust the whole thing towards her. "Take it with you."

"The whole thing? I only need the travel kit," she pointed out.

"I don't care about the bag. You might as well have it."

"Are you sure? It's gotta be worth —"

"Take it," I said firmly. "I don't need it."

"That's generous," she muttered.

But something about the way she said it made me stop.

"I'm sorry," I whispered. "I'm being a bitch, I just want to know what's going on and finding things like hospital bracelet just makes me ask more questions."

"We're going to find all the answers. I promise," Eliza said as she zipped up the bag. "I guess I should get out of here before anyone starts asking questions."

"Thank you." I gave Eliza a tight hug. Then pulled back and leveled a serious look at her. "You have everything you need. The forms? The money?"

"I have more than I need," she told me. "Wait. What about the DNA sample from Tod?" She asked.

I shook my head. "I don't think it's necessary. Everything in that bag is definitely hers."

"Are you sure?"

I stared at it. It could be another trick, something planted by Tod to throw me off track. But somehow, I knew it wasn't. This hadn't been left for me to find. I was certain that Kerrigan had hidden it. It was as if she wanted to forget it existed. "It's hers."

"Okay." Eliza seemed content to drop it. "I'll call you as soon as I have them. You sure you don't want me to stay?"

"Unless you have a fetish for funerals, I'd get out of here while you have the chance," I said dryly.

"Well, I am dying to get back to my job." We both laughed, but it was half-hearted. So much had happened during her short visit, and neither of us had processed it. There had been far too much drama and not enough girl time.

"Next time we get together it's going to be pedicures and margaritas," I promised her.

"Deal. You better get ready."

She picked up the bag, but before we reached the door, someone knocked. It was as if a timer had gone off. I was being called back to duty. They were no longer avoiding me. When I open the door, I found Giles standing in front of it with a sheet of paper in his hands.

"Let me guess. You have an itinerary?" I said, stepping to the side and doing my best to avoid making eye contact with him. Even death had a strict schedule to follow around here.

"Not exactly." He moved into the room and stopped when he saw Eliza. "I apologize. I didn't know you had company."

"It's okay. I was just leaving," she told him as she holstered the bag higher on her shoulder.

Giles glanced at the Louis Vuitton and stared at it for a moment. I could see the wheels turning in his head. He knew where Eliza lived. He knew she was a waitress like me. He knew there was no way she owned a bag like that. "Is that..."

"I gave her some things," I cut him off. "They are mine to give, right?" Disdain dripped from my voice. I couldn't hold it in. He had been part of this. He had played along with Tod's schemes. If Giles knew that I wasn't Kerrigan and wanted to stop me from doling out her possessions, he'd have to admit it. Otherwise, I had him backed into a corner.

He pushed the bridge of his glasses higher on his nose and mumbled, "Not at all. I hadn't seen that bag in a long time."

Interest swelled inside me, and I couldn't help wondering if he actually recognized it. Did he know about the hospital stay? Did he know why Kerrigan was there? It took every ounce of self-control I had to keep myself from asking those questions. The more questions I asked, the more attention I would draw to my plans. For now, no one but Eliza needed to know what I was up to. Plus, he was probably just covering for his snobbery by acting like he didn't care if she took it.

"Maybe you can see that a car takes Eliza to the train station," I suggested.

"That's not necessary," Eliza jumped in.

"Of course, it will only take a moment." Giles pulled his mobile out of his pocket and dialed the number. Eliza watched, clearly impressed as he ordered a driver to immediately bring a car to the front-drive. When he ended the call, he looked at her. "Would you like help with your bags?"

"I got this," she said quickly, her eyes darting over to me. I didn't have to tell her that that bag couldn't be let out of her sight. It was our best chance at finding out the truth about me and Kerrigan.

"Some people carry their own bags," I informed him.

"I really should go. I'm going to miss my train," Eliza said. She reached over and gave me another quick hug. "Call me."

"And you'll be back in two weeks," I asked her.

"And miss being a bridesmaid," she said wickedly. "Believe me, I'll be here."

"Oh," Giles said in a strained voice. "You'll be joining the wedding party?"

"Yes," I said, "with the date moving up, I was lucky she had availability."

Eliza bit back a snort of laughter and waved as she darted out of the bedroom.

"Do you really think that's wise?" His eyes followed her out the door.

"I'm being forced to get married in two weeks. I think you can let me have this one," I said, lifting my chin and tearing him to argue with me.

Giles paused long enough to consider and seemed to think better of debating the issue. "I have the funeral information for you. Spencer is requesting that you arrive half of an hour early to be prepped and pass through security."

"Security?" I took the sheet of paper from him. "If they're worried someone's going to kill the guest of honor, I have news for them."

His lips turned down as if he found the joke distasteful, but he didn't say anything. "Given Lord Byrd's stature within Parliament as well as his relationship with the monarchy, there will be a number of high profile guests in attendance to pay their respects. It's all on the sheet."

I scanned the paper and found my mouth dropped open. "Are you serious?"

"You're marrying into a very important family," he reminded me, his words tinged with warning.

"So everyone keeps telling me," I said as I stared at the list. There was a time when I wouldn't have expected to be in the same city as these people. Now they were coming to attend a funeral for my intended family.

"There's something else," Giles said. He cleared

his throat before reaching into the breast pocket of his jacket and withdrawing a few small books.

"What's that?" I asked.

"These are your private diaries," he said, not bothering to look up from the books.

"My private diaries?" I repeated. Why was he just giving them to me? He'd been keen to pass on any of Kerrigan's personal possessions when I arrived at Willoughby Place, so that I could pass as her. These would have been useful. Instead, he'd kept them to himself.

"You kept them hidden," he said. "I knew about them and when... Well, I thought I should hold onto them for you. I assume whatever you wrote in them you wished to remain private."

"Thank you." My mouth was dry as I took them from him. Part of me longed to open the covers, wondering what I might find inside. The rest of me wanted to shove them back into a closet under stacks and stacks of bags and clothes and pretend they never existed. But I couldn't pretend they didn't exist any more than I could pretend that I wasn't in this situation now. "I'll look at them after the funeral."

He cleared his throat. "That would be wise."

Before I could press him on his mysterious answer, the door to my quarters opened and Iris peeked in.

"I hope I'm not interrupting," she said with a cautious smile. "Eliza just said goodbye. I wanted to check in with you."

It seemed everyone wanted to make amends or whatever this awkward attempt at conversation was now.

"I'll arrange for the car to take you to Westminster in plenty of time to arrive according to the Byrd's schedule," Giles said. "Will you be needing anything else?"

"That will be it." I turned and dropped the diaries behind a pillow on the couch before waving Iris into the room. I couldn't avoid her forever. Not while we lived under the same roof, but I didn't need to share everything with her either. The trust we'd had — the friendship we had begun to form — was ruined. I would never look at her the same way again.

Iris surveyed me head-to-toe she came into the room as if checking to make sure I had all my limbs. She was dressed in black, an unusual choice for her. Usually, she wore creams and golds that set off the rich luster of her dark skin. But she was even more striking in black. The silk pantsuit moved like an extension of her. I couldn't help but stare.

No wonder she didn't wear black often. She'd probably cause traffic accidents.

"Getting ready for the funeral?" she asked as Giles took his leave.

I managed to turn my attention from her and regain my detached composure. "I suppose."

She hesitated for a moment, obviously sensing the same tension stretching between us that I felt. "I came to see how you were doing. I thought you might be more comfortable talking if we were alone."

"Why would I be more comfortable?" I asked coldly.

My words had the effect of a slap in the face. Iris took a step back before collecting herself and regaining her footing. "You have every right reason to be upset with me. Honestly, I thought I was doing what was best for you."

"By lying to me?" I asked her. "By helping Tod with this whole sham?"

"You have to understand. We were desperate," she rushed to explain. "I see now that—"

"I don't really care," I stopped her before she could run through all her excuses. None of them mattered to me. None of them excused what she had done. The Belmonds only cared about their selfish arrangements and personal desires. "Isn't the important thing that I'm here now?"

Her shoulders sagged, and, for a moment, I thought she was disappointed. Then, relief washed over her face. "All we've ever wanted was for you to be back home."

"So you can marry me off to a total stranger? Geez, thanks," I said flatly.

"If you are having second thoughts about Spencer —" Iris began.

"That's not what this is about," I cut her off again.

"And it doesn't matter. I have everything in order, so If you don't mind, I need to get ready for the funeral."

"Of course." Defeat replaced her relief. "If you need to talk, I'm here."

I knew she was extending an olive branch. She wanted to make peace. Part of me knew that she was telling the truth. She believed Tod. She was acting in my best interest in his warped version of the situation. But she had lied. She had stood by and let Tod build a cage around me and she had said nothing. She wasn't my friend. She never could be now.

"Noted." Then I turned my back on her. Just like she'd done to me.

There was security and then there was *Royal family in attendance* security. This was the latter. I hadn't known what to expect when Giles escorted me into the rear entrance of Westminster Abbey. The service was over an hour away and few attendees had arrived. No one arrived early to funerals. Who would want to? Despite the lack of guests, there were several security officers asking questions, giving pat-downs, and doing other generally intimidating things. Of course, security officers seemed like a strange term for the collection of people assembled to secure the location. I waited for a tall, broad-shouldered black man to finish speaking with an older couple dressed in funeral clothes. After he dismissed them, he nodded to an older man before turning to speak quietly with a beautiful Indian woman. They were all gorgeous. Even the older man had a distinguished air about him. They looked more like they belonged in movies instead of feeling people up on their way to a funeral. When the two officers were finished talking, the woman smirked and my eyes widened when she looked over at me with interest.

Giles stepped forward. "Miss Kerrigan Belmond, Spencer Byrd's fiancé."

I waited, unsure what to do.

"If you'll excuse me," Giles said, "I must return to Willoughby Place to see everything is running smoothly."

"Hey, Kerrigan," the black man said, waving me over with a friendly smile like we were old friends. "We just have a few questions for you. No big deal. In fact, isn't she the one..."

"The one what?" his partner asked.

"Didn't Edward say something about somebody's fiancé?"

She arched a perfect brow. "When did you talk to Edward?"

He bit his lip, his handsome face contorting with guilt.

"He's coming," he told her. "I was supposed to keep it on the lowdown. But he mentioned something about somebody's fiancé."

"Does Alexander know is coming?" she asked pointedly.

"I might have forgotten to tell him," he admitted. He turned and gave me a sheepish look that was far too much like a teddy bear for such a beast of a man. "Do you know Edward?"

I nodded, my mood brightening a bit at the thought of seeing him. I'd struck up a tentative friendship with the Prince of England while in Yorkshire. I hadn't expected to see him again so soon.

"Okay, I need you to do me a favor," the guard said to my surprise. "Don't tell him that I forgot to tell his brother he was coming. I'm pretty sure I was supposed to grease that wheel in advance."

"Okay," I said slowly.

"It's complicated," the woman informed me.

Edward had insinuated that during our time together in Yorkshire, but I kept this to myself and shrugged nonchalantly. "It will be our secret."

"Thanks," he said with relief. "Let's see, do you have any weapons on you?"

I blinked and stared at him for a moment. The change in topic had my head spinning.

"Oops, sorry. This is the part where I actually do the security," he explained.

"No weapons but my charm and wit," I reassured him.

"I like her," the woman said, half absorbed in looking over a file.

"Hey, Brex," the older man called. "I need you for a minute."

"Take over?" he asked her.

She nodded and turned her full attention to me.

Brex jogged over to discuss something with the other man, leaving me to finish my security clearance with the woman.

"This isn't exactly what I expected," I admitted to her.

"I know that he seems like a gentle giant," she said, "don't let that fool you." Her words were clipped and businesslike. Any friendliness she had shown moments before had been replaced by someone who was here to do her job. I found myself studying her more intently. While the men were dressed in suits for the funeral, she hadn't bothered with such formalities. Instead, she wore leather pants and a tailored black blazer. A lacy camisole peaked from beneath it, giving a soft edge to her otherwise commanding presence.

"I guess that's why he works for the king," I said. She asked a few more questions about my recent travels and when and where I'd been at the time of Lord Byrd's death.

"Does it matter?" I asked. "Didn't he die from natural causes?"

"Looking for consistency," she explained, dropping the cold tone she deployed during her short interroga-tion. "Yeah, the old bat dropped dead because he was ancient. But anything at Westminster...unfortunately, there's history here."

For a moment I thought she meant between the Byrds and the royal family, but then I noticed she looked around her at the church itself.

"Oh. Of course." I hadn't thought about what it meant that the king was visiting Westminster. I'm sure it wasn't the first time he'd been here since his wedding, but I doubted it ever got easier to return to this place. Not after what happened. "I'm surprised he's coming."

"Alexander knew Lord Byrd quite well. Just as I'm sure, he'll know the next Lord Byrd quite well," she said cryptically.

"Well, thanks for that," I said uncertainly, but she didn't offer more clues as to her strange comments. I was a bit surprised to hear that Spencer's grandfather had a relationship with the king. He hadn't been a terribly friendly man.

"The family will be primarily focused on speaking with visitors and attending to the matters of the funeral," she continued. "So, I'd like to ask you to keep your eyes open. There's no specific cause for concern, but, as you know, in the past security has been an issue here. If you were to see anything..."

"Of course," I said in a rush. Despite my mood, I couldn't help but feel honored to be entrusted with the safety of the attending royals.

"I'm Georgia," she introduced herself. She pointed to the black man. "That's Brex. And Norris. If you see anything, find one of us. Only one of us."

"Won't there be more security?"

"There will be, but only speak to one of us," she repeated.

I didn't press her for more information, and she didn't offer it.

It seemed I had passed whatever inspection they thought was necessary. A staff member for the Byrds ushered me to a small room where the family was cloistered before the services began. As I entered, I was suddenly self-conscious about everything I was wearing, thinking, or doing. How had I found myself here? I looked down to check my choice of ensemble and was relieved to still find it suitable. The black dress suit I'd found was fitted and formal, tailored perfectly for such an occasion. There was nothing about it that was sexy or eye-catching. It did the job of looking somber perfectly. I'd paired it with classic black Louboutins and dark hosiery. My hair was pinned into an elegant twist that I'd managed to do by myself and the Philip Treacy fascinator I'd chosen was neither ostentatious nor simple.

Spencer didn't look up as the staff member announced my arrival. He was deep in conversation with an older man I didn't recognize. But Holden's eyes darted to me and then away. I found myself deliberately avoiding him. The only person that seemed to notice or care about my presence, at all, was Evie. She rushed over and gave me a hug. "So glad to see you," she said quickly, "I felt terrible since the other night at the house. I was rude and—"

"You weren't rude," I interrupted her.

"I was. You were so nice and I acted like a brat," she said with a guilty look.

"Believe me, you're the least bratty member of your family," I whispered to her. "Have you met your brothers?"

She giggled, but as soon as it was out of her mouth, she smacked a hand over it for betraying her. "I can't believe I did that."

"I don't think anyone noticed," I reassured her. They would have to be paying any attention to us to have seen her laugh. Spencer was too busy being important. Holden was too busy being sullen. And Caroline...

"Where's your mother?"

"Probably draining her flask in the loo." Evie pursed her lips with obvious contempt. Lowering her voice, she whispered, "She's been a twat all week. The only thing she cares about is your wedding. I knew she hated grandfather, but..."

Caroline hated me, as well. I didn't understand why she cared about the wedding. Now that Lord Byrd was dead, there was no one pulling the family strings. They could do as they wanted, but both his daughter-in-law and his grandson were still following the plans he'd laid out for them.

A member of the clergy appeared in the small room, wearing ornately embroidered robes and cleared his throat politely. "We're ready for the procession."

"The what?" I whispered to Evie.

"We have to walk behind the casket and look sad," she explained. "Didn't Spencer send over the information?"

I thought of the paper Giles had brought me. I'd been too busy gawking at the guest list to read through the order of events. "He did, but I was distracted."

"Just follow my lead." She smiled warmly and directed us to follow her brothers out of the room. Before we reached the door, Caroline stumbled in.

Their mother radiated her usual poise in a charcoal-colored coat that tapered at her waist. Her silver-blonde hair was up in an intricate masterpiece with an understated hat perched on top of her curls. She looked every bit the part of the family matriarch but as she came closer, I spotted what Evie was saying earlier. Her eyes were slightly bloodshot and as she swept up to us, I caught a waft of strong juniper on her breath.

"You reek of gin," Spencer muttered to her. He snapped his fingers and one of the household staff appeared. The woman didn't seem at all put out at the condescending gesture. He whispered something to her and she disappeared in a panic. A minute later, she returned with a box of mints. "Mother."

Caroline took them timidly and hung to the side as a church official began organizing us into a line.

"First, we will have Lord Byrd's daughter here," the man said.

"No," Spencer cut him off. "My grandfather

wished for his heirs to lead the procession. My mother should walk with my sister."

The official's eyes skittered around the group before nodding. "Oh, very good."

"Kerrigan," Spencer spoke my name like an order. "You'll walk with me. Holden will follow."

Across from him Holden's jaw clenched, and he dropped his head before anyone could see his reaction. Was he upset that I was taking his place? Or was he angry over Spencer's domineering attitude? It was impossible to tell with him avoiding all of us. Regardless, he showed no sign of questioning Spencer's direction.

Caroline didn't have the same restraint. Her eyes flashed at her son. "Do you really think she should be at the front of the line?"

"As my wife, she should be at my side." Spencer shrugged a shoulder.

"You aren't married yet, son," she hissed.

"A formality," he reminded her. "Kerrigan belongs with me."

I belonged to him was more like it. Tension thickened in the room and I decided not to make it worse. I simply walked over and stood next to him.

"See?" he said to his mother as I joined him. "She understands her place."

I clamped my mouth shut to keep myself from saying something I shouldn't—especially in a church. But Holden had no such reservations.

CHAPTER ELEVEN

"You fucking wanker," he growled.

Spencer turned slowly and regarded him like he might an insect on the wall. "Maybe you should sit this out."

"You know, I think I will." Holden strode toward the exit, but his mother grabbed his arm before he reached it.

"Please," she begged. "What will people think if you aren't there?"

"No one will notice as long as Spencer is there," he bit out and continued on his way.

"It doesn't matter," Spencer said as an ancient door creaked closed behind his brother. "Let's get this over with."

Those of us remaining stayed silent as we lined up. Then after a few minutes, we were escorted to the back of the chapel where a casket waited, draped in the family crest. An arrangement of lilies covered the family motto. I strained to see it but Spencer coughed and I realized he wanted me to stay still.

The funeral was as overblown and pompous as the man had been. By the time, it was over, I was ready to leave.

"Kerrigan." Spencer crooked his arm, and I took it, relieved to finally be done. But we were far from done.

He'd meant it when he said my place was at his side. His family, save for Holden, formed a reception line near the exit to thank guests for coming. I plastered a smile on my face preparing to nod and act interested. But the first attendees to offer their condolences weren't strangers. I lit up when I saw Edward, but before I could step toward him, Spencer stepped in front of me.

"Your Majesty," he addressed his brother. "We're honored to have you in attendance."

Seeing the King of England in photographs and on television had not prepared me for meeting him in real life. If Spencer charmed the room, King Alexander commanded it. He was taller than I expected, every ounce of him well-muscled beneath his mourning suit. Even as Spencer spoke, he remained carefully distant. I'd always thought he was attractive. He'd taken his good looks from his mother, a Greek royal, who had passed away when he was a child. Her genetics had gifted him with a strong jawline and a wide, mesmerizing mouth. It was his eyes that held me captive, though. They blazed bright blue like the tip of a flame. Up close, he wasn't just handsome I realized, he was *hot*.

"I am sorry for your loss," Alexander said in a deep, sexy voice that demanded to be heard. "I suppose you'll be taking your grandfather's seat in the peerage?"

"That is the plan," Spencer said, maintaining his business-like tone.

"And if rumors are to be believed, then you'll take the prime minister's seat," the king added.

Spencer's mouth twitched. "If it is the will of the people."

"Naturally." Alexander tipped his head like he agreed.

But standing with the two of them, one the most powerful man in England and the other poised to become his equal, I knew their words were merely for show. They radiated a power that put people in their places. This was no true democracy. It was a battle for supremacy. I was reminded of what Brex, the security officer, had said earlier. Alexander owed Lord Byrd. That was why he was here. It was hard to imagine what a man like the king could need from the man.

"I'll be taking his titles as well," Spencer continued. "As will my wife." he angled his body toward me as if presenting a trophy for the monarch's inspection.

"You're married?" Alexander lifted a thick black eyebrow. "Congratulations."

"Not yet. Within the month," Spencer said.

"A word of advice about marriage?" Alexander beckoned him closer and whispered something I couldn't hear. Shock flashed over Spencer's face, but he'd carefully rearranged it by the time he straightened.

"I'll keep that in mind," he said in a strangled voice.

Alexander turned his attention to me, and I found myself pinned to the spot. There was something about him that demanded total deference. Did he have this effect on everyone?

"Best wishes on your upcoming wedding."

"Thank you, Your Majesty." I didn't know what else to say, so I dropped into a curtsy. Spencer stiffened next to me, but Alexander's mouth flattened to a line. I wasn't sure what I'd done wrong.

"That's not necessary," the king murmured, "but I appreciate the gesture." Amusement ran through his voice and I realized he was holding back a smile. I straightened as he bid Spencer farewell.

The next face was far more welcome. Edward hung back waiting for his brother to finish his condolences, but it was clear from his grin that he'd seen what happened. When Alexander moved to speak to Evie and Caroline, Spencer turned and continued overseeing their interaction with the king. Edward took the opportunity to speak to me quietly.

"How are you holding up?"

I glanced over at the others who were engaged in polite, but stiffly formal conversation. "Doing my best to make an ass out of myself," I admitted. "Thank you for coming."

"I'm trying to be better about family obligations," he said in a strained voice. "I don't think Alex knew I was coming, though."

It was strange to hear the King of England referred to so casually. "You didn't tell him?"

"It's complicated," Edward admitted. I recognized the frustration in his voice, because I had my own fair share of it.

"Is he mad at you?" I glanced over at his brother.

"Not exactly," he said, "but I think he'd rather have heard about this in advance."

I nodded, somehow understanding what he meant. Whatever was going on between the two of them expectations needed to be clear and boundaries marked. I thought of Spencer and Holden. What was it that pitted brothers against each other? "Just talk to him," I said, thinking of what I wanted for them. "Don't let whatever happened poison you against one another."

Edward's throat slid as if my words had landed harder than I anticipated. "I've decided to return to London," he told me. "But my number is the same. Call me?"

"Absolutely." I smiled widely at the thought of having another friend nearby.

"I better hurry. I want to catch up with my brother," he said, but he paused and waited.

"What?" I asked as he continued to stare.

"I was just waiting for you to curtsy," he said dryly.

I rolled my eyes at him and he leaned toward me, surprising me with a quick hug.

"Spencer, my condolences," he said to my fiancé, but Spencer was watching me with curious eyes.

"Thank you, your highness," he said coolly. Edward spoke quickly to the rest of the family and hurried after Alexander. As soon as he was out of earshot, Spencer turned to me. "Why is he hugging you?"

"Are you jealous?" I couldn't keep the surprise out of my voice.

"No." He snorted as if the thought was ludicrous. "It was just very familiar. I had no idea you two knew each other well enough for rolled eyes and hugs."

Apparently, he'd been paying really close attention, and I'd failed his secret test. "We spent an afternoon together in Yorkshire while you were gone. I forgot to mention it with everything that happened."

His eyes narrowed and then he smirked. "You never fail to impress me. Already befriending the prince. You're going to make a perfect companion when I'm Prime Minister."

I tried to smile but my face wouldn't cooperate. Thankfully, more attendees arrived to speak with us. I hung back, remaining silent, playing the role of Spencer's perfect companion. Standing here, even at his grandfather's funeral, I realized he'd never wanted to share his life with me. He wanted someone to compliment his own ambitions. I was nothing more than a beautiful object to adorn his arm. And as the minutes ticked by and Spencer spoke of me to the visitors rather than to me, I knew I was as useful to him as his wrist watch.

CHAPTER TWELVE

I'd attended a few parties at Sparrow Court since I'd arrived in London, but this felt different. The visitors gathered today spoke in hushed voices. Everyone wore black. I felt as if I was walking through shadows as I made my way to snag a bite to eat—and escape the constant introductions. Now that I was officially engaged to Spencer, everyone wanted to meet me *again*. Everywhere I turned someone who knew Kerrigan from university or charity work or rowing club cornered me to catch up. Spencer had disappeared with some lawyers to discuss important matters that couldn't wait. I suspected his grandfather would be proud that he didn't take off even for his funeral.

But that left me defenseless against the barrage of well wishers and curious newcomers. Tod and Iris were amongst the masses, but they were the last people I wanted to shield me. Evie had vanished with school friends. And Holden hadn't been seen since his dramatic exit at Westminster.

Rather than risk the buffet the caterers had set up in the ballroom, I snuck into the kitchen. The staff were too busy to notice or care that I had invaded their space. I swiped a cucumber sandwich from a tray waiting on the counter and found a quiet corner where I could hide.

I took a bite, savoring the first food I'd had all day. It was already late afternoon, not quite dinner but too late for lunch. That probably explained the afternoon tea spread. There was enough food to feed an army: sandwiches and tarts and scones and biscuits. Servers rushed out the kitchen doors and new ones dashed back inside. It was a whirl of activity everywhere I looked. By the time I'd finished the last morsel, I was eying a platter of puddings when Caroline blazed into the room with Iris by her side.

"There are two empty trays on the buffet in the parlor," she snapped at a woman stirring a bowl near the hob. "And the tea trolley needs to be refilled." She grimaced at Iris and shook her head. "You have to stay on these companies. The only punctuality they ever show is when they deliver the bill."

Iris answered with a tight smile. "I'll bear that in mind if we host any gatherings at Willoughby Place."

"You really should." Caroline turned an appraising eye to her. "People notice who hosts events and who doesn't."

"That reminds me that I wanted to talk to you about wedding plans," Iris said.

I shrank farther into the corner, wondering if I could sneak back out with some of the caterers. The last thing I wanted to think about was the wedding. Still, I was curious what they were planning. Spencer expected the date to move up. I couldn't help but hope they had encountered an obstacle in their attempts to rush the blessed event.

"With the funeral and Spencer's new responsibilities, maybe we should wait," Iris suggested.

Caroline straightened, instantly appearing taller than she had moments ago. "It's Spencer's wish that they marry as soon as possible. He's the head of this family now, so that decision is up to him."

Spencer was the one pushing to move the wedding date up? He'd made it sound as though it was his mother's obsession—a holdover from the plans for a political dynasty his grandfather had groomed him for. Why was it so important to him? And what about me? What about what I wanted?

As if she could read my mind, Iris pointed out exactly that. "Shouldn't Kerrigan have a say?"

For a moment my anger over her betrayal ebbed. Maybe she was only looking out for me. She seemed to genuinely care about me, but was that only because she believed I was Kerrigan?

"She had her say. He asked her and she said yes,"

Caroline said with a shrug as if my acceptance of Spencer's proposal was a binding legal arrangement.

"It's her wedding." Iris sounded frustrated, and I realized she must have been having this same debate for days. She'd taken my side, even though it meant losing battle after battle.

"And it will be beautiful. She'll have the wedding every bride dreams of," Caroline said dismissively.

"Perhaps, we can include her in more—"

"I don't expect you to understand how this works," Caroline cut her off, her eyes narrowing to slits. "You're new to this world. This is not simply a wedding. It is a political maneuver. It shows Spencer's maturity and will help him when he makes his run."

"Surely, he can't be planning that for at least ten more years," Iris said, tapping her manicured fingers restlessly on the marble countertop. "That leaves plenty of time—"

"The more established his family is in the public eye, the better. Ten years gives them time to marry and have children. She'll need to produce an heir and at least two more unless that American bitch pops out more little royals." Caroline chewed on each word like she could barely swallow the thought.

I no longer felt hungry. I clung to the shadows, even as part of me raged. How dare Spencer's mother plan my future like this? Was I nothing more than a breeding machine to her? Spencer and I hadn't discussed children much. Not yet. If he expected Kerrigan to immediately conceive it was news to me. But as sick as her assumptions made me, I didn't see why she was dragging the royal family into it. King Alexander had thought highly of Lord Byrd, by all accounts. He'd taken the time to come to the funeral. Spencer had been cordial to him but not friendly. All that left me to wonder what the Byrds had against the monarchy.

"What does the queen have to do with any of this?" Iris asked the question I was struggling to answer myself.

"Every time she produces another baby, the public falls more in love with the monarchy. The people are so blinded that they can't see that all power should be invested in the Parliament," Caroline continued. "My son will change all of that, but he needs to be well-loved first. If England is hungry for a handsome, young family man and his pretty wife and children, we can offer an even better version."

"Better?" Iris repeated.

"British," Caroline clarified.

There was a pause. Iris stared at her as if waiting to find out this was all a joke. "I had no idea you were so prejudiced."

"Don't be dramatic." Caroline waved off the dig. "We merely want what's best for the country. You can't blame us for that. But if you're having trouble supporting this wedding, perhaps I should speak to Tod directly."

"That won't be necessary," Iris said quickly. "I just want to make sure that Kerrigan's needs aren't forgotten in all the preparations."

"Kerrigan is the reason we're doing all of this."

"Really?" Iris tilted her and stared at Spencer's mother. "Honestly, I didn't think you liked her."

"I don't," she said without missing a beat. "But she's the result of excellent breeding and she's been groomed to step into this position her whole life. She knows her place."

Iris blinked as if she'd misheard her. "Her place? You can't actually believe that."

"As I said, our circles operate differently than the ones you are accustomed to. Women like myself or Kerrigan understand the importance of appearances and networking, but we also know how important it is to be whatever the head of the family demands."

"Like being a perfect wife and having babies?"

"It's a fair trade. She'll never know want. She'll live in the lap of luxury. What more could a girl ask for?"

A caterer interrupted them before Iris could respond. A moment later, they returned to the party, but Caroline's question lingered in my mind. *What more could a girl ask for?*

Now I knew why Kerrigan had run. Caroline was wrong. There was something she wanted, despite her wealth and privilege. It was the same thing I wanted. And it was something worth fighting for: freedom.

I made my way to the second floor, more interested in finding a private place to gather my thoughts than eating more. Caroline's words had buried themselves in my stomach, leaving a pit behind. It seemed to grow with each second. I belonged to Spencer, even Iris had barely challenged Caroline on the matter. Each moment that passed took me closer to the day when I was nothing but what he demanded of me.

The Spencer who had opened up to me was gone. There was no vulnerability. He'd stepped readily into his grandfather's shoes.

Of course, he did, I reminded myself. He's spent his whole life preparing to do just that.

But it wasn't his meteoric rise to family patriarch that left me stunned. It was the cruelness that accompanied it. I'd glimpsed his darker side before. Those instances were almost always followed by apologies. At the time, I'd written off the lapses in character. But what if the kind, funny, charming Spencer was the part he played. What if I'd given myself to a monster?

It didn't matter. When I had the DNA results in a few days, I could use them as leverage. If Tod wouldn't put a stop to the wedding, I could tell Spencer the truth. He wouldn't want the knock-off version of Kerrigan Belmond, not when he'd been offered the real thing. The only thing preventing me from doing it now was Holden.

Not my feelings for him, which were getting more and more confusing. But his insistence that Tod was telling the truth. Without proof, Tod could have me locked up for revenge, sent off to the hospital where he'd sent Kerrigan two years ago. Holden might back his claims. I wanted out of this arrangement, but not at the cost of my freedom. I couldn't risk the possibility of being placed in an institution.

I was so lost in my thoughts I didn't pay any attention to where I was heading.

"Lost?"

I whipped around, coming face-to-face with Holden. He'd abandoned his suit jacket and unknotted his tie. It hung loosely from his unbuttoned collar.

"I was just taking a moment." I cringed at how shaky my voice sounded.

"In my room?" he asked.

I looked around and realized with horror that I'd

wandered right into a bedroom. "I'm sorry," I said quickly. "I didn't mean to invade your privacy."

"I don't mind, dirty girl, and besides that, I left the door open." He nodded for me to follow him inside. I hesitated for a minute at the door, and he looked back at me. "I'll behave if you will."

I glared at him. "I'm not the one with boundary issues."

"I seem to recall you asking me to take you to bed in Yorkshire."

It took effort to pretend my face wasn't on fire, but I knew my blush was obvious. "We all have momentary lapses in judgement."

"Okay," he said with a smirk, "we'll both keep a grip on our judgement then."

I nodded and took a tentative step inside. There were books everywhere, stacked and shelved. Some lay open on a desk too cluttered to be anything more than a repository of odds and ends. A fire crackled in a stone hearth that was taller than me. A few velvet chairs were clustered around it, each surrounded by their own stacks of books and loose papers. Heavy drapes were haphazardly drawn to one side, revealing lead glass windows and allowing twilight to spill into the space. Pillows and blankets lay in a disheveled heap on a four poster bed.

"It's a mess," he said unapologetically.

"I like it," I said without thinking. Nothing was hidden here. It was laid bare for anyone to see. Everywhere I looked I caught glimpses of Holden. It wasn't the perfect living quarters I'd been given at Willoughby Place or Hensley. He actually lived here. Breathed. Thought.

"Who are you hiding from?" he asked, dropping onto the edge of his bed and propping himself on his elbow.

I turned away from the sight of him on the bed, my heart hammering in my chest. "No one. Everyone. But especially your mother."

"Where's your knight in shining armor?" he asked. "Isn't he supposed to protect you from fire-breathing dragons like her?"

"I lost track of him." I picked up a book from his desk and studied it for a moment. I didn't want to talk about Spencer. "Have you read all of these?"

"Some of them. Bits of others. My attention wanders." His free hand reached up and pulled off his tie.

"Not going back downstairs?"

"No one has missed me yet."

"That's not true." I glanced up and our eyes locked. Holden shifted, rising to his feet. He prowled closer and my breath caught. But he reached around me and picked up a decanter of bourbon. "Drink?"

I shook my head. That seemed like a very bad idea.

"So, tell me," he said as he poured the amber liquor into a crystal glass, "who missed me, dirty girl? You?"

My mouth went dry and I looked away from him.

It was easier to be honest when his eyes weren't piercing through me. "Maybe."

There was a pause. It stretched out so long that I dared to peek around at him. He stood there, drink in hand, completely frozen. "Don't fuck with me. It's impolite."

"Impolite?" I repeated, something snapping inside me. "You're always fucking with me."

"You wish." He smirked and lifted his glass to his lips. Wicked Holden was back, his mask carefully drawn once again.

"Why do you do that?" I asked in a quiet voice. "Why do you push people away?"

"People have an annoying tendency to disappoint me."

"Like Kerrigan," I guessed.

His eyes narrowed, but he didn't press the issue of her and me. "I suppose."

It had taken bribery to get him to open up to me before. I had no idea why he was being honest with me now, and too many questions I wanted to ask before he closed himself off again. Before I could stop myself, the question weighing heaviest on my mind spilled out of me. "Why didn't you go to bed with me?"

"Did I hurt your feelings?" he teased, but his eyes watched me warily.

"Never mind." It had been stupid to ask. Wasn't it bad enough that he'd rejected me that night? Why did

I want to relive it? "Where were you during the funeral?"

"I was in the back."

"You just abandoned your family," I accused.

A muscle ticked in his jaw and he placed his glass on the table. "And that was a real hardship for them, wasn't it?"

"It's not like that—"

"It isn't?" he cut me off. "Did they run after me? Did any of them come to find me and ask me to come back?"

I forced myself to see it through his eyes. Spencer had gone out of his way to put Holden in his place. That was becoming a theme with the Byrds. We were all puppets and Spencer was our master now. If Holden was conflicted about his grandfather's death before today, his brother had only made it worse. I couldn't blame him for being angry. "I'm sorry."

"For what?" he asked bitterly.

"For not standing up for you. For not coming to find you."

"I don't blame you. My brother's leash on you isn't long enough anyway."

I flinched, tears smarting my eyes. I tried to turn away before he saw, but he caught sight of my face and his own fell.

"I'm sorry."

"Don't punish me because you're angry with him," I demanded.

"Fair enough," he agreed. He sucked in a deep breath, his chest swelling out. "I didn't go to bed with you because you didn't know the truth."

I swallowed, trying to digest this information, but it sat like a lump in my throat. After a moment, I gathered my courage. "I'm getting a DNA test."

"That's wise," he said thoughtfully.

"You think it will tell me that Tod is telling the truth—that I'm Kerrigan."

One side of his mouth curved into a sad grin. "I know it will."

"And then?" My pulse pounded as I stepped closer to him and brushed my hand down his strong bicep. "What will you do if I'm Kerrigan?"

"Love you," he murmured, his eyes burning into mine.

"After everything?"

"Some things change. Some things don't." His head swiveled to the side, breaking eye contact with me.

"If you're sure..." I moved my hand to his chest, placing it in the center. His heart hammered against my palm, proof that he was affected as I was.

He covered my hand with his, his eyes squeezing shut for a moment, before he pushed it away. "Don't do this."

"Do what?" I pressed.

"Tempt me."

"You're tempted?" I asked breathlessly. "Then give in. I know what I want."

"You're still wearing his ring," he bit out, but he moved closer. His chest brushed against the swell of my breasts and desire flooded through me, pooling in my core.

"I'll take it off," I offered, tilting my head up to him. "I'll take everything off."

Holden angled his face over mine, so close that I felt his next words on my own lips. "Leave with me."

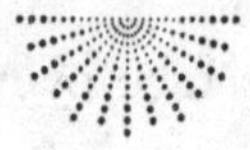

CHAPTER FOURTEEN

His words send my heart racing, but I shook my head. "I can't."

"Exactly," he said. He pulled away and walked to the door. He stood by it expectantly.

I left in a huff, equal parts frustrated and embarrassed. I found the nearest bathroom. Locking myself inside, I slipped off my skirt and touched myself. But I was too worked up to get off. I wanted him. I couldn't explain it exactly. And I knew nothing would satisfy me until I had him.

By the time I'd stepped out of the loo, I'd managed to compose myself. But even if I looked put together, inside desire raged. I wanted Holden because he rejected me. That was the only sane reason I kept throwing myself at him. Deep down, though, I knew it was more complicated than that. I was drawn to Holden, pulled to him with an undeniable magnetism that I couldn't explain. But every time we got close, he changed the rules and repelled me with an equally strong force.

That left me so pissed I wanted to scream and so turned on I'd nearly touched myself in the loo just to get relief. I'd refrained because I knew that he'd enjoy that too much. If Holden discovered I'd gotten off after our brief encounter, it would only boost his ego more. That left me with no choice but to deny myself.

Denying myself was proving harder than I expected. The relentless tick between my legs felt like a bomb that might detonate at any moment. I pressed my thighs together, taking small steps, so that my skirt barely moved. I didn't think I could handle even the scrape of fabric on my thighs at the moment. Before I could reach the stairs to head back down to the reception, Spencer appeared on the top step.

"I've been looking for you," he said, his eyes hidden in the evening shadows. "Where did you run off to?"

"I needed a minute. There's a lot of people down there." It was an easy excuse to sell because it was true. I'd trotted and pranced and performed for all of them to see.

"Tell me about it." He took the last step, bringing his full height to tower over me. "Can I tell you a secret?"

I bit my lip and nodded, but instead of speaking, he reached for my hand. Tugging me down the hall, he stopped and glanced around us, before pulling me into an empty bedroom. He didn't bother to shut the door.

"What is it?" I asked, my gaze drifting to the large bed in the center of the room.

"I spent the whole funeral thinking about fucking you," he said in a raspy voice that made me suck in a deep breath.

The pulse at my core throbbed harder. I tried to ignore it, but my body overrode my objections.

Spencer trailed a finger along my jaw. Despite everything, his touch still captivated me. "Do you want me to show you what I was picturing while the priest was giving his sermon?"

"Yes," I whispered.

Spencer tssked as if he didn't approve. "That wasn't very convincing."

He wanted me to beg like I had in the hotel. A sick realization took hold of me. When we first met, he told me that I would give myself to him. He said he would never have to take me against my will. I thought he got off on the idea of turning me on, but that wasn't what this was about.

Spencer wanted power. He got off on watching me beg, because he saw it as humiliation. He loved control, but he loved stripping mine away even more.

"Never mind," I said, stepping toward the door.

"Where are you going?" he asked sharply.

"There are dozens of people downstairs. I'm supposed to be a hostess, right?"

"My mother can handle that." He dismissed the object outright. "I want you here with me."

He did? Well, two could blame his game. "Then you should ask nicely."

His head tilted, his green eyes studying me as a slow smile spread across his face punctuated by a laugh.

"What?" I demanded

"Kerrigan has claws," he said, hooking his index finger into my suit jacket and drawing me closer. "I felt them the other night when I was fucking you, but now I see them."

"I'm sorry did I miss a please in there?" I asked him.

"Okay, we'll play your way. Can I *please* show you what I was fantasizing about? I think you'll approve." His hand slipped from my jacket and circled around my waist to fondle the zipper of my skirt. "What do you say?"

"Clothes stay on." I issued the challenge as he began to tug the zipper down.

"I can work with that." His face leaned toward mine, his breath hot on my face, and my eyes closed to welcome his kiss. He seized his chance and spun me around. He slammed me into the wall. His fingers circled my wrists and drew my arms over my head as his knee coaxed my legs apart. The tailored fit of my skirt barely gave him room to work with. "Clothes on, huh?"

"Not up to the challenge?" I asked.

He answered by shoving my skirt up to my hips, exposing the lace garter belt and stockings I wore beneath it. Only a skimpy strip of fabric covered my sex and he pushed it to the side as his fingers worked inside my slick heat.

"You're so fucking wet. Were you thinking about me, too?"

I moaned to avoid the question. All the pent-up frustration Holden left me with spilled over. Spencer accepted it greedily. His fingers slid out of me, leaving an ache behind. I cried out in frustration, pressing my cheek to the cool wall, in an attempt to soothe the ragged heat coursing through my body. The metal clink of a belt buckle sent my fraying nerves into overdrive.

"This is what I wanted," he whispered. "I wanted your pussy bare and dripping for me. I wanted to hear your body smacking against the wall as I fucked you so hard you forgot to breathe. I wanted to hear that little sigh of desperation you make when you want my cock inside you. And I wanted to do this."

His arm slid around me lifting me to the perfect angle. I bit my lip, waiting to feel his hard crown work inside me. But Spencer wasn't interested in taking his time. He drove inside me with one strong thrust. I yelped at the sudden intrusion, but he didn't pause to check on me. His palm pressed against my stomach, bracing me in place as he claimed me.

Each thrust drove away the real world. I forgot

about Caroline and her plans. I forgot about Holden's denial. I became nothing but his fantasy, and he carried me off with him.

"That's right," he coaxed, his hand sliding down until his fingers found my clit. "Come on my cock."

I did as he told me, splintering apart, as he filled me. He lowered me onto shaky legs and slid his palms down my hips. But he didn't push my skirt back into place or fix my knickers. Instead, he spread me open, making me tremble harder, and stood examining me. After a minute, he adjusted my knickers and smoothed my skirt down. I shifted to sag against the wall. I could feel his release seeping onto my thighs.

"I should clean up..." I said absently.

"No." He grabbed my chin and forced me to look into his eyes. "Leave it. I want you to remember who you belong to."

He had marked his territory. I barely heard him when he excused himself to return to his guests. Instead, I stayed slumped against the wall as I realized I could never free myself from him.

I didn't have the strength.

CHAPTER FIFTEEN

"My name is Kerrigan Belmond."

The doctor shifted in his seat and wrote something on his pad. Then, he turned his piercing gaze on me. "How does it feel to say it?"

Like a lie, I thought. "Good. Normal."

I'd agreed to meet with Dr. Simmons, Kerrigan's therapist, on the condition that he sign an affidavit that he wouldn't speak about our sessions with Tod. Everyone seemed to think it was a pointless request. Tod argued that I was already assured confidentiality. But I didn't care. I wanted it in writing. If the doctor tried to turn against me, I'd ruin him. It was as simple as that.

But now that I was here in his office, I wondered if it was enough. The entire space had been designed to calm. White on white on white with a side of white and white chairs. In other words, it was sterile, boring, and had the opposite effect. I fidgeted on the sofa and checked my watch.

He wrote another note. "And Kate?"

"What about her?" I'd practiced this part. I knew exactly what I needed to say. "She doesn't exist."

"Doesn't she?" he asked.

I shifted again and stared at my nude-leather Manolo Blahniks. I'd worn jeans and a linen blouse, opting for comfort, so I could easily lie down on the couch. Or whatever was expected of me. Now, I felt silly. It didn't matter what I wore or how quickly I jumped through the hoops. I knew the truth. I knew this was all pointless. B

"I made her up." I slipped into the lie they wanted me to believe. It was getting easier everyday. I was Kerrigan Belmond. Heiress. Engaged to Spencer Byrd, the future prime minister if he had anything to say about it.

"I see." Dr. Simmons placed his notepad on his desk and took off his glasses. "I think we're done for today."

"What?" I blinked at him in surprise. "My appointment is for an hour."

"Don't worry. I won't bill you."

I wasn't certain which was more shocking: that he wasn't going to charge me or that I was being sent away. He stood and moved toward the door.

"Am I cured?" I asked slowly. I hadn't expected it

to be this easy. I'd braced myself for a few sessions to keep Tod happy while I waited for the test results.

His forehead wrinkled, two bushy eyebrows knitting together as he inhaled deeply. "No, you're lying."

"What?" I got to my feet, daring me to say that to me face-to-face.

"You do not believe you are Kerrigan. You have accepted nothing. I told your father this would happen if you were pushed too hard too quickly." He patted my shoulder and I shrank away from him. "These things take time."

"What things? Brainwashing people?" I snapped at him. I reached down and grabbed my purse. I couldn't believe he was just kicking me out.

"There. Now that was honest," he said.

"What do you want me to say? I agreed to some crazy arrangement in exchange for ten million pounds? That I slept with a stranger while pretending to be someone else? That I'm being forced into a life of wealth that's not mine? Why would I make that up?" I demanded.

"That is what we are trying to figure out," Dr. Simmons said, bypassing my logic and returning to his previous claims. "And until you want to know those answers, we won't be able to get to the truth behind this traumatic episode."

"I'm the crazy one?" I pointed to my chest. "How is any of this helping me?"

"It's not, but you have to seek the answers."

I hadn't come all the way to South London to get five minutes of therapy. "And how do I do that?"

"We could try hypnotherapy."

"You're going to hypnotize me," I said in disbelief. Was I at a doctor's office or a Las Vegas side show?

"Regression therapy can be quite useful in uncovering past events. Think of your mind like a library. You can browse through your memories, pull them out, relive them. But there are parts of the library that are locked away, even to you. Hypnosis can help us unlock them."

"Great," I said. "So why didn't you try this on Kerrigan and fix her?"

"We have tried this before, Miss Belmond," he said gently. "It had unexpected side effects."

I crossed my arms over my chest and glared at him. "Well, now you've sold me. Do you need a pocket watch or something?"

"It was regretful," he continued, ignoring my sarcasm. "But we are more prepared to handle the episodes now."

"Episodes?" I repeated.

"The deeper we looked, the more frequently you began to experience panic attacks," he explained. When I didn't speak, he continued to clarify. "You described them as being pulled under water. I thought it might have something to do with your mother's drowning, but I underestimated the effect they were having on you."

I couldn't move. I didn't know how he'd found out about my attacks. Very few people knew about them. I'd been careful to keep them quiet since coming to London. Eliza knew, but she wouldn't tell. Holden had been there for one, but I hadn't described it to him.

"I've consulted with a colleague in Zurich and I think a different approach is warranted if you wish to pursue this avenue."

I shook my head. "No. I don't want to pursue this."

Dr. Simmons smiled sadly, nodding with understanding. I hated the pitying way he looked at me. "I'm not sure I can help you then."

"Why?" I demanded. Wasn't that his job? Why couldn't he just listen? Why wouldn't he allow me to convince him that I was telling the truth?

"Because, my dear, you don't want to be helped yet."

I slammed the door to Willoughby Place behind me and raced up the stairs. I'd been waiting for Eliza to call me, but I couldn't wait any longer. I wouldn't. I'd grab my bag—the one I'd brought with me from West Bexby—and get a bus back to the one-pub village. My job would be waiting for me at the Hare and Hound. Eliza would let me crash while I figured things out. I didn't care about my arrangement with Tod or my engagement to Spencer. I didn't want any money from them. I only wanted my life back.

Rounding the corner to Kerrigan's room, I discovered a crew of men carrying boxes out of it.

"What the hell is going on?" I demanded from one of them.

He nearly dropped the box, barely managing to right his grip before it crashed to the floor. "I was hired to help move some things. That's all I know."

I stepped to the side and let him pass, knowing the poor guy wasn't to blame for what was happening. But who was? I waited for another mover to carry a box out before I walked in to find Giles and Iris overseeing the process.

"Did I miss something?" I asked.

"Oh, you're home!" Iris smiled brightly, but as she looked at me, her cheerful mood faltered. "What's wrong? Did things not go well at the doctor's?"

Things had not gone well, but I wasn't about to admit that. Plus, there was the much bigger issue of Kerrigan's life being packed up and taken away. "What's wrong? Why are you packing up my room?"

Iris and Giles shared a look. She took a cautious step forward. "We assumed you knew about this. The movers showed up after Spencer called."

"Spencer?" I repeated in a strangled voice.

"Yes, he said you were moving into Sparrow Court. With the wedding so soon, I didn't think anything of it. He didn't ask you?"

"No, he didn't," I said through gritted teeth.

"I'm sure he assumed it was okay," Iris said, but I tuned out her excuses.

Everyone knew what was best for me. They were all acting in my best interest. No one bothered to consult me, at all. No one cared what I wanted. I twisted Spencer's engagement ring around my finger. I'd been prepared to leave London behind, but this time I wouldn't run. They'd lied to me, manipulated me, and robbed me.

I wouldn't leave here empty-handed. I wanted answers. I wanted revenge. I would face my captors, one by one.

Starting with Spencer Byrd.

I took the steps down two at a time, but before I reached the bottom of the stairs, Tod Belmond appeared in the foyer. His face was white as if he'd just seen a ghost. I paused, noticing an envelope clenched in his hands.

"This arrived for you," he said in a strained voice and held out the letter.

I took the last few stairs slowly, unsure I wanted to take it. Whatever it was, it had upset him. He passed me the envelope. It was addressed to Kerrigan Belmond, and my heart stuttered when I saw the return address. I flipped it over, surprised to see it was still sealed.

"You didn't open it," I said.

"I don't have to open it." His hands remained balled at his sides.

If he hadn't seen what was inside, why was he so upset?

"Go on," he urged.

"Maybe I should..." I don't know why the laboratory had sent a letter to me. I'd put Eliza's address on the forms. Now I was on the spot. I could open the envelope in front of Tod or I could try to bluff over its contents. Truthfully, I didn't know what was inside.

"Open it," he demanded. "I want to see your face."

I could feel my pulse in my fingers as I broke the seal. The room grew hotter as I withdrew two pieces of paper. I unfolded the top one.

Attn: Kerrigan Belmond,

Per request, please find a copy of your receipt.

It was a receipt. They'd sent a copy to the billing address I'd entered for my card. But my relief was short-lived when I read the following sentences.

A copy of your test results has been included for your files.

I didn't look up. I couldn't find the strength to lift my head. But I felt Tod's wary gaze on me as I sifted the sheets and read the second sheet of paper.

There were two columns for each sample followed by numbers and words that meant nothing to me. The only thing that stood out was that each line was exactly the same. My heart stopped when they reached the final lines.

Probability of match: 100%

Based on the DNA samples provided, our laboratory has confirmed they came from the same individual.

The paper fluttered to the ground, my hands unable to hold its weight. I stared at where it had fallen. Everything felt numb.

"You really didn't know," Tod finally broke the silence.

A tear rolled down my cheek. I didn't look up even as more fat, hot drops followed.

"Perhaps we should call Dr. Simmons," he suggested.

I shook my head. There was too much to process, but I wasn't ready to face the therapist again. Everything he'd said was true. I searched for an explanation for the results.

"How do I know you didn't tamper with them?" I asked in a shaky voice.

"Do you really think I'm so desperate to fool you that I would lie to my own daughter?" Sadness echoed in his voice, and I turned my gaze up to face him. He stared back at me, his face etched in worry. It was the face of a father.

My father.

Why didn't I recognize it?

"I don't know what you're capable of," I admitted to him in a small voice.

"Everything I've done is for you." He swallowed, turning his head to try to hide the tears shimmering in his own eyes.

I couldn't remember my past. If the results were to be believed, I was Kerrigan. But no matter how hard I sifted through my memories, I couldn't find her there. There was something else, though. Something that turned my blood to ice.

Nothing.

No childhood. No schools. Just flashes of moments without context, too chopped up to make sense of. The first concrete moment I could recall was riding on a train and deciding to get off at a stop marked West Bexby.

I couldn't remember any more of me—of Kate. But I couldn't remember Kerrigan either. Questions swam into my head, each demanding to be answered, before being replaced by a new, more pressing concern. But one kept swirling around and forcing its way to the front of my mind.

"If that's true, if you're only thinking of me, why are you making me marry Spencer?"

"It's complicated," he said, his eyes darting away

"What's new?" I muttered.

"Kerrigan, please, you need to trust me."

I flinched at the sound of her name. "Why should I trust you?"

"Because I'm protecting you," he said. "Marrying Spencer will keep you safe."

"From what?" I sobbed. All the pieces were laid before me, but they still didn't form a picture. I didn't know how they ever could.

"I made a deal after your mother's accident," he admitted in a low voice. "Questions were being asked. There was going to be an inquiry."

"It was an accident," I said, repeating his own words.

"Not everything added up to that," he said. "I couldn't let them look into more, so I struck a deal with Lord Byrd and he made it go away. If you call the wedding off, Lord Byrd ensured the inquiry would be reopened, even after his death."

"Why would he do that?"

"Our money will help Spencer's party get the majority in the general election and keep that power. Lord Byrd believed it would help Spencer rise to leader of his party more quickly if his family's money was putting MPs in their seats. Once you're married, he'll be able to finance as many campaigns as are necessary."

I was a bank account to the Byrds. Nothing more.

"I don't understand," I said slowly. "Why would you be willing to give him that much money to avoid an investigation?"

"It's better if the accident remains an accident," he said darkly.

"Are you saying someone killed her? Tried to kill me? Why would you cover that up? To protect your reputation? Was it you?"

I'd never asked questions about that night. Now it had come up two times in one day.

"No, I didn't kill your mother," he said sadly. "I think you did."

CHAPTER SEVENTEEN

He didn't stop me from leaving. I didn't bother with the test results, but as I climbed into the Porsche I scrounged up the courage to call Eliza.

"Hey, I was just going to call you," she said when I picked up.

My stomach twisted into a knot. "Oh."

"Your test results arrived," she said. "Do you want me to take the train up and bring them to you?"

I closed my eyes, pressing the phone so hard to my ear that it hurt. "Just open them."

"Are you sure?" She sounded uncertain.

"Yeah."

"Okay, drumroll." Paper rustled on the other end of the line then it went silent.

"Eliza?" I prompted after a minute.

"Fuck," she whispered. "I...I'm sorry."

I didn't wait for her to tell me it was a match. "I'll call you later."

I hung up the phone before she could ask questions or try to soothe me. Ten minutes had changed my life into one I didn't recognize. I flipped open the car's visor and inspected myself in the mirror. I knew the face staring back at me. Nothing else. My skin was splotchy from tears and my eye make-up smudged. I dabbed at it with my fingers to fix it. The redness would fade.

I stared at my reflection. "Who are you?"

Was I a killer? I'd never thought I'd ask myself that question. There were things I knew now. Indisputable facts. I was Kerrigan Belmond. I was engaged to Spencer Byrd. I was worth billions. These facts were like tent poles, propping up the makeshift identity I'd been forced to inhabit. Now I needed to build something solid on them.

Because I had to marry Spencer. I couldn't remember my past. Maybe I was a murderer. Maybe I was responsible for my mother's death. Tod had agreed to the marriage to protect me. He'd traded a life in prison for one in a gilded cage.

There was no other choice.

And what would happen to Tod if there was an investigation? Would he get in trouble for trying to cover it up? Would it ruin his life? Would it ruin Iris's? I hated him for protecting me at the cost of my freedom, but could I sacrifice all of them to prevent this marriage?

I would become Kerrigan Byrd, but I wouldn't allow Spencer to dictate every decision in my life. He couldn't move me into his house without asking. He couldn't order me around like he owned me. I would marry Spencer, because I had to, but I would not be his puppet.

CHAPTER EIGHTEEN

Boxes were stacked inside Spencer's flat when I arrived. Outside the windows, night crept over the city, vanquishing the remaining daylight. I stared at the half-packed apartment. Apparently, I wasn't the only one moving. Of course, I had expected him to live at Sparrow Court, especially after his grandfather's death. But part of me was surprised that he was giving up his flat. A stack of boxes came walking down the hall, stacked so high I couldn't see who was carrying them. I skirted out of the way just as Holden squatted to put them near the door.

"Hi," I said feeling a bit shy.

He glanced up, momentarily stunned. "I didn't know you were here."

"I just got here." I dropped my keys on the counter and looked around. "So Spencer is moving into the house."

"Apparently, our bachelor pad days are over," Holden told me bitterly.

"Wait, you're moving, too?"

"He sold the flat. Spencer feels there is more than enough room at Sparrow Court for all of us."

My mouth fell open, numbness spreading over my body as I realized what he was saying.

"Don't worry, dirty girl." His voice was sharp. "It's a big house. I'll stay out of the way."

Before today, I never thought it would come to this. I'd believed I would prove I wasn't Kerrigan. I believed I could walk away from this life. I'd barely begun to process that this was my world, like it or not, or that I had no choice but to marry Spencer. But with each second, my cage constricted a little more.

"Why would he want..."

"You're not the only one he wants to keep an eye on. He can't have any of us screwing up his reputation within his party," Holden explained.

I shook my head. This wasn't happening. I'd accepted my fate, but I couldn't allow Holden to suffer, too. "You don't have to do this. You can leave."

"We all have strings," Holden said, "and he's holding all of them."

"I'm going to marry him."

"Were you having second thoughts?" Holden took a step toward me, and I fought the urge to close the gap between us.

"I can convince him it's a bad idea," I whispered.

"How are you going to do that?"

I had no idea, but there had to be a way. "I'll do whatever I have to do."

"I can't let you give any more of yourself away." Holden tucked a loose strand of hair behind my ear.

"What about what I want?" My face tilted up, daring him to deny me.

Holden's eyes searched mine, before widening. "Kerrigan?"

"If the DNA tests are to be believed," I said softly.

"What do you believe?" His voice caught on the words, snagging on something that sounded painfully like hope.

"I don't really have a choice. Facts are facts."

"You're not understanding me. Who—"

"Exactly what's going on between you two?" Spencer cut him off, angrily.

I stepped away from Holden, willing my face to remain blank. I wouldn't give fuel to his accusation. But Spencer glared between us, his face darkening like the shadows growing around us.

"Nothing." I tried to move past him, but he caught me. I yanked my arm free. "You're being ridiculous."

"Ridiculous?" he repeated the word, and I cringed at how it sounded on his lips.

But there was no turning back from this now. It was way too complicated to explain to him, even if I wanted to. I had no idea how much Spencer knew about my father's arrangement with Lord Byrd. Had his grandfather told him? How would he feel to know my father had purchased a reprieve for me? Would he look at me differently if he knew I might have killed my mother? Would he believe I was guilty? I wasn't prepared for Spencer to have an opinion.

"I'm not blind. You two are hiding something," he accused.

"You might not be blind, but you're paranoid." I crossed my arms, refusing to give in to his accusations. "And why didn't you ask me about Sparrow Court?"

"We can talk about that later," he said harshly. "Right now, I want to know why you and Holden are suddenly so close."

"This again?"

"I should go," Holden broke in. "Text me when she's gone, so I can finish packing."

"Answer me, dammit!"

Holden's shoulders squared and he turned to face him. "I promised you I wouldn't touch her without your permission."

He did? I stared at him, rawness creeping up my throat. Was that why he kept refusing me?

"But you want to," Spencer said.

"I don't have time for this." Holden moved to push past him. "She's yours. I know that."

His words stung, and I fought the urge to cry.

"Wait." Spencer stepped in front of the door, barring his brother from leaving. "Prove it. Prove she's mine. Go to bed with us. Now. Tonight."

I wasn't sure which one of us he was talking to. Was he asking me to go to bed with them? Or Holden to join us? Was I asking myself stupid questions to avoid the fact that it didn't really matter?

Spencer's gaze answered the first question for me. He wasn't looking at me but past me to where Holden stood, ready to leave.

He was asking him. Not me. He didn't need to ask me because he assumed I would do whatever he said. Spencer might not know all the details of the arrangement that had bound him to me, but he knew he owned me, all the same.

I stared at him. Then I turned my head slowly to look at Holden. It was like turning between mirrors. Wary determination etched their faces. Neither would back down from this challenge now that it had been issued. But Holden couldn't say yes. He wouldn't.

Holden met my eyes. "What do you want?"

I dropped my head, hopelessly searching for a way out of this situation. "I don't see what this proves."

"Everything," Spencer cut in, his words as sharp as a blade's edge. "If he comes to bed with us, it will put a stop to this little flirtation. My brother has been punishing me for keeping you to myself."

I couldn't bring myself to look at Holden to see if this was true. "And what about me? What about what I want?"

"Don't you understand yet?" Spencer stepped closer to me. Pressing a finger to my chin, he tilted my face up to meet his eyes. "You want what I tell you to want."

It felt as though a trap door had opened under my feet. My stomach plummeted along with every romantic fantasy I'd ever had about us. Spencer Byrd didn't love me. He never had. He never would. I wasn't certain he was capable of love. I was nothing more than the jewel in his collection, the pet he kept at his side. I'd known I was exchanging one prison for another. In this light, the gilded bars of Spencer's cage looked tarnished. How much worse would it be after we married? Would he clip my wings? Would he let me out to fly when he could watch me?

It was a test. Not just for Holden, but for me. No matter how I answered, I would lose. There was no way to pass his examination. Refusing might make him press his thumb harder to my back until he broke me. Saying yes would only make things worse between him and his brother. I couldn't make the right move. I just had to do what I wanted. I had to think about myself and my own needs and desires. I had to find pleasure in my captivity.

Turning my head away, I slipped past him without a word, without a glance, and walked toward the bedroom. No footsteps followed me, so I wasn't surprised when I pivoted around to find them both watching me on the other side of the doorframe.

I kicked off my heels, then raised an eyebrow impatiently. "Are you two going to fuck me or what?"

CHAPTER NINETEEN

Spencer wasted no time accepting my invitation. He strode into the room, stripping his shirt off as he came. My eyes skirted over his bare skin, drinking in the tight stacked abs and defined pecs. He was a monster, but he was beautiful. I'd taken a step into the unknown, and all I wanted now was to feel his skin on mine along with Holden's. Spencer stepped behind me, his hands circling around my waist, and began deftly unbuttoning my top. But Holden didn't budge as his brother undressed me before him.

Our gazes locked, and I saw the battle waging inside him. It had been easy for Spencer to walk in here and claim what he believed was already his. Watching Holden, I realized it wasn't about staking his claim. It never had been to him. It was about me and what I wanted.

It always had been about me.

There was only one way Holden would come in here and join us. Maybe he didn't believe I was making this choice. I couldn't blame him for that. For all intents and purposes, it looked like I was simply doing as Spencer instructed. Maybe he was just in shock that I'd finally accepted the truth.

But this wasn't about Spencer. It wasn't about Holden.

There was an itch inside me. It had started in the loo at Hillgrove's, and it wasn't getting any easier to ignore. I'd considered going to bed with Holden, but I realized now that he would never go to bed with me behind his brother's back. That would have been accepting a scrap of me. He wanted more. Maybe he didn't think I could give him more with Spencer here, but I was determined to prove him wrong.

"Please," I mouthed, a silent entreaty for him alone. "I need you."

The last time I'd said those words to him, he'd sent Spencer in his place. I'd thought it was cowardice. Now I recognized it as something else: chivalry. Holden might toy and flirt, but he had accepted that I was out of bounds. Only I could prove otherwise.

Holden cocked his head, still puzzling out what to do.

There was only one card I had left in my hand. I'd never wanted to play it. I was never certain I could because it wasn't a bluff to throw it down. It was going all in.

It was easier for my lips to form the words than I'd expected. I'd been so afraid of them for so long. Maybe it was why they made no sound as they left my tongue. Maybe it was just wishful thinking. Maybe I'd never considered that I might mean them.

I love you.

Holden stiffened, his body going completely rigid. For a minute, he didn't move. He didn't even breathe. Questions formed in his eyes, replacing the turmoil with confusion. I smiled one final, unspoken invitation.

He angled his body as if to turn and walk away. Spencer's lips found the curve of my neck as he slipped my shirt from my shoulders. I stifled a gasp of pleasure and kept my eyes on Holden.

Only a few minutes ago, I'd thought I wanted him to escape. Now I knew the truth. I would take whatever scrap of him I could have. I'd invite him into my cage. I'd sing for him and my captor as long as they played with me.

There was a moment of hesitation before Holden shifted on his feet and started into the bedroom. Whatever reluctance he felt seemed to fall away with each sure step he took inside until he reached us and bent to capture my mouth with his.

This kiss was different from the stolen ones. It was real. He tasted sweet like the first bite of fruit after it's finally ripened. I'd waited for him. I'd resisted him. At last, it was time. His hands gripped my shoulders, squeezing softly as if to remind me that I still had a choice. I moaned to let him know what I wanted, and his fingers skimmed down the straps of my bra and glided over its lace cups. My nipples hardened at the teasing contact, and he pulled away, dipping his head to take one in his mouth.

"How does she taste, brother?" Spencer asked, his hand slipping past my waistline, down the front of my jeans and inside my knickers. He pushed a finger between my folds, and I groaned with pleasure.

But Holden didn't answer his question. He moved to the other breast, dragging his teeth across the pebbled flesh pressing against its lacy confines.

"I think he likes you," Spencer murmured in my ear. His words tingled like drops of icy water down my neck. "How could he not? You are the most perfect woman we've ever had. I've been dying to see him worship you."

I closed my eyes, banishing the questions his words raised. I chose to believe them instead. I chose to believe I was perfect in their eyes. I chose to let them worship me. I kept them closed until a hand unzipped my pants. Looking down, I discovered Holden on his knees. He gazed up at me with hooded eyes as he hooked his thumbs into my waistband and pulled my jeans to my ankles. Spencer's arms tightened around me as Holden helped me carefully out of each of my shoes. My pants followed. Every inch of my skin was on fire. I'd been naked with them before, but not with Holden's face hovering so close to my navel. He watched me as he drew my knickers down my thighs, past my calves, and then off entirely. My teeth sank into my lip as I savored the thrill of exposure. Holden leaned forward and buried his face into me, taking a deep breath.

When he finally sat back on his heels, he only said one word, "Exquisite."

"Isn't she?" Spencer stroked his palm in circles on my backside. "You should taste her."

I whimpered, wondering if I could come just from words alone.

"Shhh," Spencer soothed me. "You need that, don't you?"

I swallowed and managed a nod.

"I'll tell you a secret," he whispered as I grew dizzy between his coaxing hands and Holden's warm breath tickling my nether regions. "Holden is a gentle-man. You're going to have to ask him for what you want."

Another whimper escaped me. I didn't think I could find the words.

"It's a lot to process," Spencer said. "I understand. Repeat after me. *Please.*"

"Please," I breathed.

"Good." He brushed a strand of hair behind my ear and continued, "Now the rest. *Please fuck me with your tongue.*"

I nearly choked as desire swelled in my throat. I clenched my eyes closed, shutting out some of the stimuli around me. "Please...fuck me with your tongue."

"Gladly," Holden's gruff voice answered. Warm hands gripped my inner thighs and urged my legs open wider. My left foot was barely planted on the floor when his mouth closed over the bare skin between my thighs. He sucked me into his mouth before pulling back just long enough to thrust his tongue past my seam. My knees quivered at the confident assault, and I found myself sagging against Spencer's strong chest. His hard cock pressed into my backside, still contained by his pants, but promising me more pleasure to come. I felt his hand slip up to cup my breast as Holden's fingers pried me open to give his tongue better access. I was so caught in the moment that I hardly noticed Spencer's other hand slide gently between my cheeks. His fingers pushed lower, dipping inside me as Holden's tongue stroked me up a never-ending staircase of bliss. Then Spencer slid his fingers free, and I ached from their absence until I felt a fingertip circle the tight pucker of my ass.

"Ohhhhh," I cried out as he encouraged the digit in farther.

"Does it feel good?" he murmured, pushing in a little deeper.

My answer came in a strangled sob. It was too much and not enough. I wasn't sure I liked it, but I didn't want him to stop.

"That's right." He kissed my neck and began to

pump his finger gently. "Relax. We're going to make every inch of you feel good. You're going to come again and again until you're soft and wet and ready for both of us."

Holden planted his mouth over my increasingly engorged clit, focusing entirely on it. At the same time, his brother played with my ass and made filthy promises. I kept climbing, but now I could see the top. I'd nearly reached it. My limbs tightened, my pleasure still pinned to some unknown point.

"And then I'll watch you ride him before I bury my cock in your ass. That's what you want: both our cocks deep inside you." His words released me as he kissed the back of my neck, and I flew, tethered only to their hands and mouths, toward the sun until every part of me burst into flame.

And for a moment, I was free.

CHAPTER TWENTY

"Easy," Spencer called me back to earth as he steadied me on my feet. "Get on the bed."

He had to help me since my legs were too shaky to climb onto the mattress. I collapsed into a heap like a rag doll.

"I think she enjoyed that," Spencer said, his voice sounding far away.

"I know I did," Holden added, and a thrill rushed through me. "I think she might need a minute."

I tried to respond, but it only came out as a soft whine.

"You might be right," Spencer agreed with a laugh.

My eyes were finally beginning to focus, and I tilted my head just enough to watch him continue to undress. I shifted my head and found Holden watching me with cautious eyes, still fully closed. I lifted my arm, reaching for him but finding myself still too weak to move.

"I think she's trying to tell you something. You want to return the favor, don't you?"

I tried to nod. I'd kept my hands off Holden long enough. I'd told myself no. Now that I was here with both of them, I would take everything I denied myself.

"Let me help." Spencer leaned over me, brushing a possessive kiss over my lips before he wrenched my body toward the edge of the bed. My head fell over the side when he'd pulled my shoulders to the very edge. "Open your mouth so we can give you what you want."

I did as he instructed, my eyes skirting over to see that Holden had begun to strip finally. Maybe if I searched long enough, I would find a freckle that differentiated the two of them. But as Holden revealed more of his body, I marveled that not one perfect specimen of man existed but two.

And tonight, I got to have them both.

Spencer didn't wait for his brother to finish undressing before he stepped closer and brought himself to my lips. I let my head relax back farther, accepting his length deep into my throat. He plunged in and out for a minute, muttering dirty promises until he withdrew and stepped to the side.

"Enjoy," he said to Holden, half permission, half warning. The message was clear. Spencer was sharing me in his mind.

But it didn't matter what he believed. I turned my

eyes to Holden, pleading silently for him to take me. I licked my tongue over my lower lip to show him what I wanted, and he moved closer to bring the crown of his cock to my lips. I wrapped my tongue around it in encouragement, savoring the way he tasted. His eyes shuddered as I reached up and grabbed his length to guide him in.

I closed my eyes and sucked his cock, wanting to make him feel as good as he made me feel.

"Kerrigan," he grunted, and I snapped back to reality. "Stop before I come."

But I wanted him to come like he'd made me come.

"Look how much she wants it," Spencer interrupted. "She's a born cocksucker."

A shadow clouded Holden's eyes, and I sensed a storm forming. I released him instinctively and moved to my hands and knees, hoping I could distract them both.

"How does this work?" I simpered, throwing a come hither look over my shoulder. I was on all fours, but it was empowering to see them standing there, wanting me.

"I think you need to come a few more times," Spencer said.

"I don't think I can wait another minute," I murmured. That part was true. I felt trapped in my own skin as if the real me was trying to claw free.

"Do you have a preference?" Spencer asked Holden, who hadn't looked away from me yet.

"Bottom," he muttered.

"Letting me have her first there, too. Always the gentleman." Spencer clapped him on the shoulder and turned to retrieve something from the dresser.

A muscle ticked in Holden's jaw, but he didn't respond. He walked toward the other side of the bed and sank onto it, his back against the headboard. Lifting his fingers, he beckoned me to him. "Come here, dirty girl."

His words sounded casual, but I heard the current running through them.

I crawled forward, but he stopped me. "Should I get protection?"

"She's on the pill now," Spencer called over his shoulder while he rifled through the top drawer.

But Holden's eyes asked me the question again.

"No," I whispered. "I want to feel you."

He flinched slightly as if my response physically pained him before he nodded.

"Fuck," Spencer said, and we both turned to look at him, our bodies still keeping a careful distance. "Get her warmed up while I find the lube."

He disappeared into the bathroom, leaving me alone with Holden. Neither of us moved.

"You don't have to," Holden said flatly. "I can put an end to this."

"How?" It was one word with so many questions attached. How could he stop what they had started together? How would he smooth this over with Spencer? How could we walk away?

But I didn't want him to answer. I continued to him, lifting my leg to settle over his lap, and took his face in my hands. "I want this. It's the only way I can have you. Let's steal this moment while it's ours."

I lowered my mouth to his, knowing it was risky to kiss him when Spencer might walk in and see. But I didn't care. Holden gripped my hips and guided me gently down until my body welcomed him inside me. A cry tore through my chest as I joined him.

I'd finally discovered the difference between him and Spencer. It wasn't a freckle. It wasn't anything I could see. It was something I could only feel.

It was everything.

I rocked against him, and his arms slid up and folded around me, pulling me closer. All the questions I'd asked myself since that day in the pub fell away. None of it mattered. I'd found what I'd never lost in his arms.

And then it was taken away with the stroke of a finger down my spine. Holden broke our kiss, our eyes meeting for only a moment before he plastered his smug mask into place.

"Take long enough?" he asked Spencer.

His brother's finger continued down to my tailbone, then farther.

"She's too tight to do it without this."

His finger was slick as he pushed it inside me. My

body betrayed me, and my eyes rolled back as the intrusion shifted to a fullness I hadn't known was possible.

Holden's fingers dug into my hips, concern lighting his eyes. "Are you sure you want this?"

Spencer stilled as if waiting for my answer. I was on the cusp of having them both, but was that what I wanted? Could I handle it? Shouldn't I feel ashamed? But even as I considered his questions and my own, I couldn't deny how I felt.

Alive.

Powerful.

Electrified.

I wasn't giving my body to them. I was taking theirs. I was the one in charge. I had total control over everything that happened between the three of us. It was up to me to decide how much I could take, and I wanted more.

"Yes," I said, looking Holden directly in the eye. "I want to know what you both feel like inside me."

"Thank God," Spencer said, sliding his finger in and out once more. "I need to fuck you."

Holden tensed beneath me, the shift in his mood nearly imperceptible. I leaned to kiss him, lingering longer than I should before he broke away. The mattress dipped as Spencer joined us.

"Put your arms around my neck," Holden murmured, and I did as he suggested. I buried my face into his shoulder as he rolled us onto our sides. I looked up with surprise at the change in position, and he explained, "It's easier this way the first time."

Holden slid a hand down and urged my leg up over his hips before he drove his cock back to its root. Hard flesh pressed against my back as Spencer molded his body against mine. His hand moved down to my ass, his fingers more slippery than before, and I realized he was getting me ready. Then it disappeared, and I felt the hard tip of his cock nudge against me.

"Nice and slow," Spencer promised and kissed my shoulder.

I nodded to no one in particular. My teeth found my lower lip as I braced myself. Spencer shifted and pushed in an inch.

"Ouch!" I yelped as my body protested the intrusion. I whimpered. This time from pain, not pleasure. "It hurts."

"Give it a second," Holden said in a low voice, "or tell us to stop."

I swallowed. "Don't stop."

"That's my girl," Spencer chuckled behind me. "She knows that we're going to make her feel good. Now relax a little."

That was easier to say than to do with two brutally perfect men breaching my body. Holden kissed my forehead, and I felt some of my tension ease.

"That's right." There was approval in Spencer's voice, and I felt his shaft slide in further. "Nearly there. You're doing so well. Isn't she?"

"Perfect," Holden murmured, but his eyes told a

different story. They'd grown savage as my own body calmed, as if the storm had moved on to him.

Spencer grunted as he pushed the rest of the way in, and I gasped. It was agony. It felt as if I might split in two. Part of me wished I would. Then I would never have to choose between them. I wouldn't have to pretend. I wouldn't have to be the perfect wife, in love with the wrong man. But there was only so much I had to give. Even now, I felt stretched too far.

There was something else, though. I was full. They had filled me in a way only this moment could. I'd hoped for a way to unite them and heal their relationship. Now I knew that I was the key all along. I was the bridge that joined them. I understood now why they did this—why they took women to bed together. But this was different. I sensed it. The bridge we'd built had to burn. We all knew that.

"Come back," Holden whispered. "Be here."

The storm in his eyes had died, wiped away by a fire I'd never seen before. It ignited inside me, turning my core molten as I lay full of them.

"You're so fucking tight," Spencer groaned. "How does it feel?"

I closed my eyes and lost myself to the sensations crowding me. I felt like I might explode. I felt pulled and anchored. I ached in terrible but wonderful pain. I let a moan slip from me. "So good."

"We're going to fuck you now." Spencer's warning carried a dark edge that made me tremble.

"Carefully," Holden ordered, and I knew he was talking to his brother, not me.

And then they began to move.

I'd never known pleasure until that moment. There was no moment of absence as they thrust. One drove into me while the other retreated. The cycle was endless. Pleasure replaced pleasure, and every few seconds, they'd meet in glorious union. I tightened around them, my nerves humming until there was nothing but ecstasy. It seeped through my body in an unrelenting deluge. There was no time to crash down before another wave swelled within me.

In their arms, I was rewritten into something primal and raw. There was nothing else but this. I didn't need anything else. I only wanted the moment to last forever as I rode the endless pleasure.

"That's right," Spencer coaxed, slamming harder into me and momentarily breaking the spell. "Tell us how much you love it."

"I love it," I moaned, my head lolling dreamily between them as they pistoned relentlessly inside me. "I love you."

A palm slid under my head, and Holden lifted it. His mouth covered mine, and I wanted to weep. He knew that I meant what I said. I felt it in his kiss. But he also knew I'd stay like this forever, caught between the two of them. Another hand pressed to my cheek and drew me away from his lips. I didn't have time to protest before Spencer turned my face enough that he could angle his own over mine. He crushed his lips to my mouth possessively as though to stake his claim. But instead of fighting him, Holden brought his mouth to my chin, kissing along my jaw until Spencer pulled away and allowed Holden to capture my lips again.

They kissed me and fucked me until I no longer knew which hands belonged to which man, which lips were on mine, which greedy fingers stole across my breasts. They were mine entirely, giving themselves completely.

"Fuck," Spencer groaned, and heat spilled inside me.

I opened a bleary eye and looked at Holden, who wore an expression of grim determination, and he continued to pump. Spencer withdrew, and I whimpered, but before I could beg for him to fill me again, Holden flipped me onto my back and pinned me to the bed, rolling his hips slowly and languidly.

"Ask me," he urged. "Tell me what you want."

"Come," I begged. "I want to be full of you."

A groan roared from him, followed by long, hot lashes of climax.

He pulled out, and I couldn't think of anything but them inside me. My hand moved down to touch their seed, and I closed my eyes as I felt the hot proof of their climax weeping from me. Without thought, I spread it with sticky fingers up to my engorged nub and began to circle furiously. I felt their eyes on me as I took control of my pleasure again. They'd given me everything they had, but I wanted more. My limbs shook as I worked myself into a frenzy and exploded one final time before going limp on the bed.

Silence followed, and then nothing.

CHAPTER TWENTY-ONE

I'd never felt so sticky in my entire life. I opened one eye a crack, peeking blearily at the massive fortress surrounding me. Holden was turned to me, snoring softly, his face pressed to my rib cage. On the other side, Spencer was sound asleep, one calf thrown casually over mine like an anchor. It was like being surrounded by two furnaces. I wiggled carefully free of them, my sweaty skin slipping free easily. I tiptoed to the bathroom and dealt with the aftermath of a night spent with not one but two men.

Yeah, I was a train wreck.

Turning on the shower, I sought refuge under the hot water. But I couldn't wash away the confusion I felt about the night before. I could still feel their hands on me, their skin on my skin, their lips worshipping me. It was the most erotic experience of my life. I didn't want to erase it, but I wasn't sure how to process it.

Because I'd given in to my most selfish desires. I wanted to go to bed with Holden and I was willing to pay the price. I hadn't expected to want...*more*. But my body ached with an emptiness I didn't understand. I knew why I went to bed with Holden, but if I'd hope it would satiate my desire for him, I'd been wrong. But Spencer had done nothing but show the darkness he'd hidden since we met. Looking back, I saw all the clues. I'd been blinded by his charm and promises. I should hate him. I certainly didn't like him much anymore.

But I had no doubt that if he walked in here and carried me back to that bed, I would give myself to them in every possible way.

That's why I could never let it happen again. One taste would haunt me. Another might destroy me. I could become addicted to the way they made me feel.

I had to go cold turkey.

The door to the loo slid open, and I wiped away fog on the shower door, trying to determine who had joined me. Between the steam and the water running into my eyes from my wet hair, I couldn't tell.

"You can stay in there forever, but you'll never be clean, dirty girl."

Holden. My core clenched. I closed my eyes and tried to get my body under control. I had to marry Spencer. I knew that now. I also knew I couldn't go to bed with both of them again. But that was the only way I could have the man I wanted.

"Holden," I called his name. "I'm almost finished, and—"

Before I completed the thought, the door slid open and he stepped inside.

Oh holy fuck.

My resolve vanished like the steam rising from the hot water. It just sort of fizzled and faded. I drank him in, my eyes skimming down his godlike form. He moved closer and I caught my breath.

"May I?" he asked, tilting his head to the water.

The shower was just big enough for both of us, but I pressed closer to the wall. He stepped under the water and let it cascade over him. Droplets snaked along his skin, running in the dips and ridges of his sinewy body. I watched as he lifted his powerful arms and began to shampoo his hair. He was a work of art, and I couldn't stop staring. If he'd woken with an erection there was no proof of it now, but that didn't make his cock any less impressive. Without thinking, I reached and took it in my hand, spurring it awake.

"Kerrigan," he said in a strained voice, his hands stilling on his soapy hair.

"Shhh," I coaxed him. "Don't say anything."

I leaned in and kissed his shoulder.

"But..."

"It's okay, *Spencer*." I said the name meaningfully. How could anyone prove it was anything other than an honest mistake?

"This isn't—"

I cut him off with a kiss and his resistance melted away with the water washing over us. It was long and lingering. Holden explored my mouth and I welcomed every lash of his tongue over mine and every slight nip of his teeth. He shifted me back against the tiled wall, dipping down to kiss my nipples. When he lifted his face to mine, a hurricane raged in his green eyes. His hands scooped me off my feet and I curled around him.

"Tell me to stop," he said gruffly as his cock nudged against me.

"Never stop," I urged. My arms circled his neck, bringing him to me, but before our lips could meet, a bemused cough interrupted us.

"Am I interrupting?"

I peeked over Holden's shoulder, doing my best to look natural when I said, "Good morning, Holden."

The hands gripping my ass dug into my skin when I lied, but I ignored him.

"Holden?" Spencer repeated. Then he laughed. "You bastard."

"What?" I blinked and then turned wide eyes on the man who held me now. "Wait..."

A muscle ticked in Holden's jaw, the storm still brewing in his eyes, but he tossed a smirk over his shoulder. "You can't blame a guy for trying."

Spencer stepped into the shower and I went weak in Holden's arms.

"Whoa, dirty girl." He hoisted me up again, but

this time he carefully angled his body so that less of us touched.

"I think we wore her out last night." Spencer stepped closer and leaned in to kiss me.

I whimpered as his lips touched mine, savoring the sensations each provoked in me.

"Of course, she looks like she wants more," he said, glancing at his brother.

"I might have worked her up a little," he admitted.

Spencer nodded. "Just ask next time."

There was a pause before Holden agreed.

"You got her?" Spencer asked him.

"Always." But he was looking at me as he said it. His hold on me tightened and he turned me back under the water. I clung to him, but his strong body showed no sign of letting me fall. Spencer moved behind me. With my legs around Holden's waist, I was completely exposed and Spencer slid his hand along my sex. His fingers pumped in and out and my body strained toward Holden wanting more contact—more of everything.

Spencer kissed my earlobe and whispered, "Do you want us again?"

I'd made up my mind to say no, but crushed between them, their cocks pressed against my slippery flesh, I changed my mind. Giving in one more time wouldn't be a problem.

I could stop whenever I wanted to.

CHAPTER TWENTY-TWO

My room at Sparrow Court was smaller than I was accustomed to, likely because it was attached to Spencer's quarters. But it was by no means cramped. A four-poster bed occupied its center, complete with upholstered drapes that could be drawn for privacy. On the far wall, a fire was lit in the Italian marble hearth. Two built-in bookcases sat empty on either side of the fireplace. Other than the furniture and linens, there were no personal items or decorations in the room.

I took it all in quietly while Caroline watched from the corner with hawkish focus.

"Your clothing has been hung in the closet," she told me, pointing to a door. "At least as much as they could fit in it. The rest is in the guest room at the end of the hall."

I wasn't certain what to say, so I just nodded.

"You can arrange with Spencer to convert one of the rooms to a larger space." She smoothed an invisible wrinkle in her silk blouse.

"I'm sure that won't be necessary."

"You haven't seen the size of the closet," she said pointedly. "Regardless, you can use any rooms you wish."

I turned and sized her up. She was more put together than she had been at the funeral. Her blonde bob was coiffed to perfection, her makeup flawless, and her ensemble elegant. The only scent wafting from her was slightly too much Chanel No. 5. But though she looked the part, something about her had changed. I couldn't quite put my finger on it.

"Which room would you like me to use?" I asked. If I was going to live here peacefully, I needed to be respectful as much as possible. This was her home. I didn't want my presence to feel like an invasion.

"My dear, after next week, you will be mistress of this house. There's no point in asking me what I want anymore." The brittle words were bitter, and I realized that she didn't see my arrival as an invasion. In her eyes, the coup had already taken place, and I had won.

"But I care," I pressed. "I want us to get along. All of us."

Caroline chuckled humorlessly, pushing her hair behind one ear. She looked around the room and smiled, but the gesture was as empty as her laugh. "What you want is irrelevant. With both my sons here, there won't be any peace. You've walked into a night-mare. We can't escape it."

"There has to be something..." I trailed off. I didn't want to admit that I agreed with her. Spencer's decision to force us all under the same roof felt like a recipe for disaster, especially after I'd spent the night with both him and Holden. "Can't we find a way to make it better?"

"Not for us. I've already enrolled Evie in Yardsdale. She leaves after Christmas."

"You're sending her away?" I asked. My heart ached at the thought of losing the only perpetually friendly member of the Byrd family.

"It's for the best," Caroline said, her tone leaving no room for discussion regarding the matter. "Her brothers have a tendency to wreck everything in their path. It's always been that way."

"They aren't children anymore," I said, even though I suspected she was right.

"And that makes them even more dangerous," she warned me. She shrugged her petite shoulders as if to say *what can you do*. "You'll want to hire your own lady's maid. I would prefer to keep mine unless you'd rather she work for you."

"That won't be necessary," I stopped her forced deference. "I have Giles."

In fact, I hadn't actually discussed him coming with me to Sparrow Court. I wasn't sure I wanted him to or that he would be amenable to the idea. After discovering he had conspired with Tod and Iris to trick me into returning home, I didn't trust him. But it wasn't like I could trust anyone I hired.

"It's not appropriate for you to keep a male assistant," she said.

I couldn't believe what she was insinuating. Clearly, she had never met Giles. "There's nothing to worry about."

"A lady's maid—"

"Belongs in a Jane Austen novel," I interrupted her. I'd struggled enough with the idea of an assistant. I couldn't imagine what I would do with a maid. I imagined sitting in a chair while she braided my hair and I gossiped about the neighbors. That wasn't the life I wanted. "I suppose as mistress of the house, it's up to me."

Her lips flattened into a tight line as if she was holding back a cutting remark. When she finally responded, her words were carefully measured. "Spencer won't like it."

"I guess it's a good thing that he's not working for Spencer," I said hotly.

"You still don't understand, do you?" she said, laughter spilling from her. "You might be the mistress of the house, but Spencer is the king."

"Spencer is going to be my husband," I reminded her. "We're equals."

Caroline stepped toward the door, and for a moment, I actually thought I'd won the argument. But she stopped short of leaving. She placed one manicured hand on the doorframe and turned a wicked smile on me. There was no false deference or feigned politeness. It was pure poison. "He might marry you, silly, arrogant girl, but you will never be his equal."

She left me in my new home, her words hanging in the air, as inescapable as the truth behind them.

CHAPTER TWENTY-THREE

If my welcome had been awkward, dinner was even more uncomfortable. I arrived to the table promptly at seven per the instructions I was given. Instantly, I felt out of place. The rest of the family had dressed for dinner. The men wore suits. Caroline had traded her silk blouse and pressed pants for a long-sleeved floral gown. Even Evie, who was by far the least formal, had opted for a pink dress topped with a cream cardigan.

No one had told me that dinner was a formal affair. I looked down at my yoga pants and worn t-shirt from Oxford , which must have been from my university days, and felt even more out of place.

I'd spent the day unpacking Kerrigan's life into my new home and trying to find pieces of myself in the boxes that had been delivered from Willoughby Place.

It had been a fruitless and increasingly frustrating exercise. And now I'd shown up to my first day as future mistress of the house in stretchy pants that were covered in a patina of dust and cardboard.

Spencer stood as I entered the room and pulled out my chair. He had taken the seat at the head of the table, looking like he had belonged there all the time. My seat was now positioned on his left. Caroline sat opposite me, Evie by her side. No one sat at the other end of the table, which meant Holden occupied the seat to my right. I was more than surprised that Spencer had placed us next to one another. Maybe the other night had finally vanquished his paranoia regarding my relationship with his brother.

But as the first course was served, it became clear that we were playing a game of musical chairs. Was this how it was always going to be? The four of us vying for the coveted place next to him. Would any of us ever take the seat opposite Spencer as his equal?

"Holden, I'd like you to come into the office next week. I will need you on hand while Kerrigan and I are on our honeymoon," he said, piercing a leaf of lettuce with his fork.

"You can't be serious?" Holden dropped his fork on the table and swiveled to face his brother. "Why me?"

"I want someone I can trust there." Spencer continued eating as if this was a completely normal request.

Except it wasn't, and everyone at the table knew it.

"Since when am I someone you can trust?" Holden pressed.

"You're family."

"That's a low bar," Holden muttered.

"Darling, you can't really think that's a good idea," Caroline interjected. She'd yet to touch her plate, but her wine glass needed to be refilled.

Holden smirked, looking vindicated and insulted at the same time. "Thanks for the vote of confidence."

"You know what I mean," she said with a dismissive wave before she lifted her hand to snap her fingers. A server appeared and refilled her chardonnay.

"Not really." Holden lounged in his seat and tugged at his tie. "Elucidate me."

"That won't be necessary," Spencer said, ending the bickering. Then, he turned his attention to me.

There was a time when I might have melted under the intensity shining in his green eyes, now it made me shiver. Was this what it would be like every evening? Would we line up to receive our orders over dinner?

"I need you to meet me tomorrow afternoon," he said.

Before I could ask why Evie pushed her chair back and stood. She dropped her napkin on the table.

"Give me a kiss before you go," Caroline said.

Evie started to lean down to kiss her mother's cheek, but Spencer cleared his throat.

"It's dinner," he said meaningfully.

"Oh, um, I have plans with some friends," Evie said, biting her lip, still bent slightly over. "I cleared it with mum."

Spencer lifted his own napkin and dabbed his lips. "You didn't clear it with me."

Evie glanced at her mother. Caroline, meanwhile, was clutching her wineglass so tightly her knuckles were white. I half-expected it to shatter.

"I said she could go," Caroline said, managing to sound calm even though she was visibly unnerved.

"And I said that it's dinner time," Spencer replied. His eyes locked with his mother's, and everyone went totally silent. Holden didn't move, but his gaze followed the quiet battle being waged.

"Let her go," I spoke up, reaching for my own glass of wine. "She's going to be so caught up with the wedding next week that she won't have time for any fun."

"I had no idea fun was such a vital part of life," Spencer said, not breaking eye contact with Caroline.

"That's pretty obvious," Holden grumbled.

"What was that?" Spencer finally looked away, pinning his murderous stare at Holden.

"Just because you wasted most of your life being miserable doesn't mean Evie has to, as well." It was clear from Holden's tone that he had some experience in the matter.

Spencer said nothing. A server came to clear the plates. Another delivered the second course. We all waited. Evie still hovering nervously near her mother. Caroline finished her second glass of wine. And Spencer and Holden remained locked in their never ending skirmish.

This was how it was going to be. When Caroline warned me about how things would change at Sparrow Court, I thought she was exaggerating to scare me. But it was worth more than I ever imagined. I couldn't live caught between the brotherly rivalry, nor should Evie. I even felt sympathetic toward Caroline. Was that what she'd endured since she came to live here after her own marriage?

"Go, Evie," I commanded in a clear, resolute voice. "Just make sure everyone knows when you have plans in the future, please." I looked at Spencer. "Is there anything you would like to add?"

He seemed to struggle to unhinge his jaw. When he finally spoke, his voice was filled with barely filtered rage. "Don't be late."

"Okay," Evie chirped. She bent and pecked her mother on the cheek before racing out of the room.

I couldn't blame her for wanting to put as much space between herself and whatever might happen next. But Spencer didn't explode. He simply picked up his fork and continued where he left off.

"As I was saying, I need you to meet me tomorrow."

"Of course." I swallowed, knowing there was no way I'd gotten off so easily. "What for?"

His mouth crooked up like he was savoring the news he was about to deliver. "To sign our prenuptial agreement."

CHAPTER TWENTY-FOUR

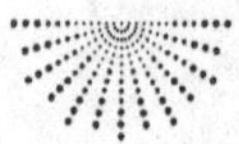

I went to bed alone that night, locking the door to my room. I needed space to think, but sitting amongst the unpacked boxes—the remnants of my former life—I was only reminded of how terribly things had gone wrong. I was doomed to live my life in this hellish house caught between a man who wanted to possess me and one who wanted to love me. I couldn't have one without the other, which left me with the distinct feeling of having neither.

My thoughts turned to the night we shared together. Even then, they had sought to lay claim to me, but it was the closest I'd ever come to seeing them unified. Is that what it would take? Is that why Spencer had demanded we live under the same roof? And if it came to going to bed with them to contain their rivalry, would I?

A gush of heat between my legs answered for me.

But this time, shame accompanied it. My body wanted the pleasure they promised, but I couldn't ignore Spencer's treatment of his family or his treatment of me. Could I really overlook the iron fist he'd clenched around all of us because of what he could do with his cock? Alone, I felt like I could, but that strength seemed to evaporate in the heat of the moment. He knew that and that's why he persisted in pressing all my buttons.

But he wasn't here now. Was he in his room?

My thoughts shifted to Holden, imagining him drinking alone in the billiards room. Last night, they'd been inside me. I closed my eyes and I could still feel their touch. My fingers drifted to my mouth, recalling the taste of Holden's kiss, while my other hand slid to the ache between my legs.

I was sore from the experience, but I didn't care. Maybe if I could sate this hunger inside me, I could keep a clear head when I faced them. But even as I touched myself, I knew it would never happen. My body was conditioned to respond to their presence. Even thinking of them seemed to jumpstart my hormones until I was drenched and desperate.

I fell back on the bed, rubbing myself harder, trying to push the throbbing bundle of nerves toward release.

"Stop that," Spencer's harsh voice interrupted.

I froze, my hand still down my pants. Part of me was embarrassed to be caught in the act, then I remembered everything we had shared. Spencer wouldn't make me feel ashamed for my pleasure. He could take my freedom. He could take my hand in marriage. But there were parts of me he would never own. I wouldn't allow it.

I closed my eyes and continued. I was so close, and knowing he was here, being forced to watch but not touch pushed me closer.

I heard him walking to the bed, and I circled faster, trying to escape before he caught me. I was near the edge, the precipice in view when he yanked my hand from my pants.

"What the fuck?" I screamed at him, panting and sweaty.

"I told you to stop," he repeated, his eyes dark pools of black in the dim lighting.

"You don't tell me what to do," I said, tugging free from him.

He laughed, shaking his head slightly. "I only wanted to watch."

"Newsflash: you were watching," I said, frustration getting the better of me.

"Don't be like that," he coaxed. He took my hand gently, and I resisted the urge to draw it away from him. I watched as he lifted my fingers to his lips. One by one, he took each one into his mouth and sucked.

My core turned molten, my arousal taking over my brain. Spencer released my hand.

"Continue," he said softly, "but take off your pants."

"On one condition," I said, fighting the instinct to immediately comply.

"I'm listening." He leaned back against the bed, his back supported by its thick poster.

"You have to watch, no touching."

Intrigue flared in his eyes, but he considered for a moment before he nodded.

I hooked my fingers around my waistband, and he moved to help me.

"No!" I held a hand. "No touching. In fact, I want you to give me some space."

"Kerrigan," he said my name like a warning.

"That's the deal. Otherwise, the door is that way." I shrugged, hoping he wouldn't call my bluff.

Spencer stalked to the armchair in the corner of the room and lowered himself into it.

I gulped back the apprehension I felt and finished taking off my yoga pants and knickers. But as I reached between my legs, Spencer coughed.

"Yes?" I bit out.

"I can't see," he said simply.

I restrained myself from snapping back at him. He was the one who had walked in on me. His interruption had left me dangling one foot over the edge of a cliff. But despite my annoyance, I wiggled around, scooting my ass to the foot of the bed. I wanted him to see. That was the point. Spencer thought he could control me. I wanted him to see exactly how out of his control I was. I widened my legs, revealing my naked sex to him, and pushed a finger into my slick heat.

I felt his gaze on me. He couldn't touch me, but he was fucking me with those dark, cruel eyes. Sensation took over. I let my head drop as I fucked myself in front of him. I imagined Holden's mouth on me as he knelt between my legs. The heat of his tongue as he licked my sensitive flesh. I recalled how he spilled inside me. My breath sped up, my fingers working faster. But then I wasn't imagining.

A wet tongue lapped between my legs, and my eyes flew open. Spencer's head was between my legs in clear breach of our no touching agreement. Still, I didn't care because he was whispering the secrets of the universe to my swollen clit, and I never wanted him to stop.

My hands fisted into the sheets, and I bucked harder against his mouth. My body tightened, each nerve winding round and round and—

Cool air shivered across my wet skin, the heat of Spencer's mouth gone.

"Wh-what are you doing?" I struggled to find the words. I twisted the sheets between my fingers as my hips wriggled with frustration.

Spencer leaned over the bed, his strong arms bracketing my body. I arched toward him, but he didn't budge. Instead, he swept his tongue over his lips as if to savor my flavor.

"Don't ever contradict me again," he ordered. "Enjoy your evening."

"You son of a bitch." I let the sheets go and reached for a pillow to lob at his head.

But he was already to the bathroom door, returning to his attached quarters. I threw the pillow anyway but missed. It crumpled to the floor as I fell against the bed, too angry to finish what he had started.

CHAPTER TWENTY-FIVE

The Byrd family employed enough lawyers to fill an entire floor of the Gherkin building in London's financial district. I'd come armed for the occasion in a tightly-fitted red dress. Despite its long sleeves and high neck, it was enough but modest since the skirt stopped a scandalous inch below my bare ass. I'd paired it with sky-high Louboutins in nude leather, making it look as if my legs went on and on forever. Under, I'd chosen a delicate mesh thong with a matching balconette bra in the same attention-grabbing red.

I sauntered into the office like a piece of bait. But while I might look like blood in the water, I was the shark. Spencer could manipulate and tease all he wanted, but I had the money he needed to exact his plan to gain power in his party. Without my wealth, he would never rise high enough to become Prime Minister on his ambitious timetable.

He could marry me, but I wasn't going to sign over anything without approving it. I might not have come to grips with who I was or my family's status, but I wasn't a fool either.

"Miss Belmond," an older woman caught my attention from her seat behind the reception desk. She blinked as she took me in but did a decent job of hiding her disapproval of how I looked. I could almost see her thoughts flashing over her forehead in lights:

Gold digger.

Of course, that's what she thought. I couldn't blame her. I wouldn't even be here if it wasn't partially true. Money had lured me into this trap. But what she didn't know was that I was the one that had it. Spencer Byrd was the gold digger. I smiled politely and nodded my head.

The smile fell from my face when she showed me into a conference room. Spencer was waiting along with a few men who must be the family lawyers along with Tod.

"What are you doing here?" I asked, instantly losing my composure.

"Gentlemen, may I introduce my lovely fiancée Kerrigan Belmond."

I forced a polite hello and turned an expectant look on Spencer. He wasn't going to use etiquette to avoid my question.

"Your father is here to finalize the financial aspects of the prenuptial agreement," Spencer explained.

"Is that necessary?" I accepted a seat from one of the partners, crossing my legs as he laid a contract in front of me.

"This marriage is as much a financial union as a romantic one."

If that was true, we wouldn't be here at all. I kept the thought to myself as I began to read the prenuptial agreement. By the end of the first page, my stomach was churning. By the second, I might vomit. When I reached the clause outlining the delivery of *heirs*, I pushed it away entirely.

I blinked as tears pricked my eyes, determined not to let any fall. "You want me to sign this?"

"That's the point," Spencer said coolly. "Is there a problem?"

"Where do I begin?" But I'd expected as much from Spencer. Part of me thought this would be about protecting his familial assets and family name. How naive. This was about getting his hooks into the Belmond bank account forever. I turned to look at Tod. "Did you read this?"

I understood why Tod had made this arrangement years ago, even if I disagreed with his decision. But even though he felt like a stranger to me, he saw his daughter sitting at this table now.

"You have to understand—"

"If party B—that's me, by the way—fails to

conceive within fourteen months, both parties agree to initialize fertility treatments immediately." My voice cracked as I read the contract language. "Should I go over the timeline of my pregnancies? You're going to have a lot of grandchildren to look after."

"Children are part of a happy marriage," Spencer said in a firm voice.

"Is that so?" I raised an eyebrow. "What about full access to my trust fund and all future inheritance, guaranteed by my father? Is that a necessary ingredient, too? Are you sure you don't want him to throw in a few chickens and a goat?"

There was no way out of the contract. Even if we divorced, he would retain a significant portion of my assets.

"Don't be dramatic," Spencer said.

"Party B will cease the usage of all contraception following the legal declaration of their marriage," I read to him before I tossed the contract on the table. "What about my demands?"

"Kerrigan," Tod said carefully, but I ignored him. Maybe he was doing this to protect me, but he had no idea what was truly at stake.

"You have demands?" Spencer said, steepling his fingers.

"I do." I stared at him across the table.

"Gentlemen, can I have a minute with my wife?"

"Future wife," I corrected him. "We haven't said I do yet."

And I hadn't signed his bloody contract either.

The others stood and poured out of the room. Tod paused beside me. "Maybe I should stay."

"I don't think that's a good idea."

I'd never been more keenly aware that I was in the presence of my father—even a father who felt like a stranger to me—than right now.

"If that's what you want..."

I nodded. He left the room with a sigh and closed the door behind him.

"You're upset," Spencer noted.

"Thanks for the update." I poked the stack of papers with my index finger. "Do you really expect me to agree to this?"

"You already have," he said with a bemused smile.

"I didn't know I was greeting to put my uterus on a schedule."

"You had time to decide, and you chose my offer of marriage," he pointed out.

My mouth fell open, and I scrambled to close it again, angry that he'd caught me so off-guard. "We went on a few dates, and you proposed. This is something else entirely."

His eyes rolled slightly, and I was grateful he was across the table because my palm itched to slap him. "You know how this works in our circles. Why are you acting like this is unusual?"

I understood why I'd run now. I'd felt the walls closing in on me. I'd known there was no way to avoid these expectations. I hadn't escaped it then. How did I expect to now?

"I'm not entirely unreasonable," Spencer continued. "You'll have access to a spending account that would make the queen blush. If you want nannies, that can be arranged."

"What if I don't want children?" I asked.

"Don't be stupid," he snapped. "People like us need heirs."

"So, let's wait. We can have an heir ten years from now."

"That's not possible."

I expected his response because of the conversation I'd overheard between Iris and Caroline. This wasn't just about lineage or the family name. Children would help in the eyes of the public as well as within his own party.

"I know it sounds daunting," he said gently like he was trying to coax a frightened kitten to his palm, "but you can have everything you want. *Everyone* you want."

I stared at him, a horrible realization dawning on me. "What?"

"Both of us." His throat slid. "I'm not blind. You can deny it all you want, but there is something between you and Holden. At first, I was jealous, but I'm past that now."

Laughter bubbled up my throat. "Oh really?"

"Do you remember how you felt pinned between

us? You were wild. I've never seen a woman climax like that. Do you remember how you touched yourself after? You can have that all the time, even..." He cleared his throat, adjusting his tie a little before he finished his offer. "Even when I'm not around."

"What are you saying?" He couldn't be implying what I thought. He wouldn't.

"I can be generous," Spencer said, "especially when I am obeyed."

"Are you telling me that I can fuck your brother as much as I want if we follow your rules?" I spit the words at him. Nausea surged through me again.

But he didn't flinch at the accusation. "Yes. Provided that you continue to visit my bed or share yours with both of us."

"Like one big happy family?" A hysterical edge gripped me. This couldn't be happening. My head began to spin, icy water lapped my feet. Not now. I couldn't lose it in front of him now, not with everything at stake.

I forced myself to focus. This was lunacy. I just had to get him to see it. "What about your baby timeline? You want me off the pill next week, remember? How will Holden feel about that? How will you feel?"

"Why would that matter?" he said curiously.

"What if I...what if Holden..." I struggled to even ask the question.

But Spencer had thought of this, too. "We're identical, remember. It hardly matters which one of us gets you pregnant. We'd never be able to tell anyway." He shrugged like this was a completely normal aspect of marriage. "I imagine with both of us sharing your bed, we'll conceive in no time."

I fought the urge to drop my head, knowing that if I looked down, I would be sick. It felt as if I'd been tossed from a boat. Each word that left his mouth battered me like strong waves.

I pushed my seat back, leaving the contract on the table unsigned. "I can't...I just..."

"Yes, you can," he said coldly, "and you will."

"You can't force me into this twisted game of yours." I stood up, discovering my knees were shaky.

"Can't I?" he asked. "I know about my grandfather's arrangement with your father. I know about the investigation and about what you did. I think I've been very understanding given that you ran away instead of fulfilling your duty. I even gave you a choice in the matter."

For a moment, I stared at him in mute shock. "H-h-how long?"

"I've always known," he said with a shrug. "It's not a problem unless you make it one."

"I didn't do anything, so if you think you can force me to marry you—"

"Let me be clear," he said, cutting me off. "Sign that contract or that investigation opens. I can bury your family in tabloid gossip, drag things out in court."

"Go ahead." I met his gaze. "I won't marry you to avoid a scandal. I don't care if you ruin me."

"Ruin you?" he said. "There's no one I can't touch. Your father. He won't have a pound when I'm through with him. Iris has some delightful skeletons in her past that the tabloids would be interested in. And then there's Holden..."

"You wouldn't," I breathed. "He's your brother, and you need to keep your family name clean."

"Everyone has to remove the scum sometimes. He's done so many terrible things that people will thank me for disowning him."

"Stop," I said through gritted teeth. "I'll sign your fucking contract. I'll do whatever you want."

Spencer slid a pen across the table and grinned.

CHAPTER TWENTY-SIX

"I'll admit that I was surprised when you called," Dr. Simmons said as he took the chair across from mine.

I fidgeted in my seat, trying to ignore how foolish I felt being back here after everything. The last time I'd seen him I'd practically called him a liar. "I wasn't ready to listen before."

"And that has changed since the results of your test?"

I nodded with a quick swallow. "I want to know everything."

"One thing at a time," he said, jotting something on his pad of paper.

"Look, I'll level with you. I don't have time to waste." I wasn't entirely certain what I hoped to get out of another session with Dr. Simmons. But doing something had to be better than waiting to give my soul away to Spencer this weekend.

"I see." He peeked over his glasses at me. "Why don't we start with why you're here, Miss Belmond?" He paused. "May I call you that?"

"Yes," I murmured. "I'm getting used to it."

"That may take some time. You must protect yourself while you heal from this experience."

"I wish I could," I confessed.

"I believe you are suffering from a dissociative identity disorder."

"What does that mean?" I asked.

"Some trauma or pressure has essentially caused you to create a new, safer reality. You believed you were Kate. I could see that, even if others remained unconvinced. You felt safer as Kate."

"Kate was an orphan on the run from...I don't even know what...with no money or friends."

"Exactly," he said. "Your parents and your wealth don't make you feel safe. You felt threatened rather than secure."

"So, I went crazy? Isn't that extreme?" Why couldn't I just have binged some ice cream or actually run away to the Riviera? Both sounded like healthier, and much easier, options.

"The disorder likely stemmed from an actual event. When I first met you, I was certain you were suffering from some acute, long-ignored trauma."

"Like what?"

"It's impossible to say. The regression therapy was supposed to give us answers, but it seemed to aggravate your situation more."

"And if we try it now?"

"I believe it would make things worse not better," he said apologetically. "Is there a reason you've changed your mind?"

I told him about Spencer and the wedding, filling him in on the details of the prenuptial agreement. He listened without comment. "Since I signed the contract, I've felt the pull of an anxiety attack."

"How often?"

"Every waking hour." I dropped my head in my hands. Sleep was my only respite, but even that didn't feel safe. Spencer hadn't visited my room since we'd signed the contract a few days ago. He'd been busy preparing to whisk me away on a romantic honeymoon. "I've been to see the seamstress and oversee little details, and I don't care about any of it. I just want it to be over with."

"You sound as if you are having second thoughts about marrying Spencer?"

I snorted. "You could say that."

"You didn't anticipate the expectations for your marriage, like children?"

I shook my head. Until recently, children had felt a long way off. Now I was expected to be a mother within two years' time. How could I do that when I didn't know who I was. I told Dr. Simmons this, and he stayed silent for a moment.

"Perhaps you should call off the wedding," he said gently. "It seems that you are not as committed to this union as you should be. Honestly, I was hesitant to force the issue, but I feel your best interests need to be considered."

"There's something else," I admitted. Up until now, I hadn't been sure I could trust his motivations, but for the first time, I realized he cared more about me than his hourly rate. "Everything I say here is confidential, right?"

"You have the expectation of privacy unless you are planning to harm yourself or someone else," he tacked on thoughtfully.

"Nothing like that." My mouth felt dry, like it was stuffed with cotton. Could I really tell him everything? *Everything everything?*

He seemed to sense my hesitation. "Being honest might be exactly what you need to find your way out from this situation. I promise I won't judge."

I wasn't so sure about that. To his credit, the doctor barely batted an eye as I filled him in on every sordid detail. That I'd agreed to Tod's scheme, that I'd lost my virginity to Spencer, that I'd gone to bed with him and Holden. It tumbled out of me like leaves caught in a windstorm.

When I finally finished, he tilted his head thoughtfully. "You're leaving something out."

I shook my head. I'd told him everything. I'd confessed it all—down to every last filthy detail.

"How did you feel about Spencer when this relationship began?" he asked.

"Curious." I couldn't think of a better word. I'd tumbled down the rabbit hole and fallen into his upside-down world before I questioned how I could find my way out.

"And Holden?"

"Curious," I repeated.

He tipped his head, biting back a bemused smile. "I apologize. I'm not judging you. I imagine if I was in your shoes with two beautiful women vying for my attention, I would be torn."

"That's how it started." And now everything was more complicated than I could have imagined.

"Perhaps, but let me ask you, what about now? How do you feel about him?"

"I love him." It slipped effortlessly from my mouth. Dr. Simmons raised an eyebrow, and I rushed to clarify. "Holden. I love him. I don't understand it, exactly. I feel like it's always been there. Maybe somewhere deep down, I remember him. But it's impossible..."

"Anything is possible if you remove the *I'm* standing in the way." He leveled a severe gaze at me. "Do you want to know what I think?"

That was why I was here. I nodded, waiting for him to find the missing key. The one that would unlock everything.

"You must give in to these panic attacks," he said.

I sucked in a breath. "I can't."

"Can't and won't are different animals," he said in a gentle voice. "Kerrigan, I believe this started when we tried regression therapy."

"That's why I'm here now. I want you to hypnotize me or whatever. Figure out what's wrong with me. I accept whatever risk that carries with it." And if he couldn't do that, he could convince me to let all of this go. I would let him feed me whatever lies were necessary to live in this strange world.

"It's not that simple, or we would have had success before. Your mind is already trying to help you see what's wrong," he explained.

"It's doing a shit job." My voice cracked.

"No. It is doing what it can. The rest is up to you."

"I'm trying." Why couldn't he see that? Why couldn't anyone see that? My family, the doctor, Holden—they all wanted answers. But none of them wanted them more than me? None of them were willing to go as far as I would go to find them.

"And that, my dear, is your problem. You have to let go. Give in to the panic. Let the memories overwhelm you. That's where you will find your answers." He paused before delivering the bad news. "But, Kerrigan, you might not like what you discover."

CHAPTER TWENTY-SEVEN

The next day I found myself staring at the gown hanging from the wardrobe in my new bedroom. It wasn't the dress I'd chosen in the shop. There'd been no time to rush its order. Its loss was a small mercy. I couldn't bear the thought of wearing that dress to exchange vows with Spencer. I never wanted to see it again.

I felt nothing for the strapless gown we'd managed to find. The dress itself was pretty. Covered in delicate lace, it tightened to a sheath at my hips before puddling into a small train. Given the weather, the bridal salon had suggested a fur cape to wear as well. I smiled when everyone gushed and pretended I was pleased. In a way I was. It meant that my dream dress wouldn't be worn as I walked into a nightmare.

A knock at the door signaled the arrival of Camille and her crew.

"Oh," she exclaimed as she came into the room and looked at the dress. "Your gown is beautiful!"

I forced a smile. "Let's see what you can do about the rest of me."

She clucked with disapproval at my self-degradation and set about preparing me for today's photoshoot. Caroline had moved heaven and hell to get a photographer here to do a bridal portrait before the wedding at Spencer's insistence.

"This will be a trial run, yes?" Camille asked as she debated between two pots of pink blush. "It will give us a chance to change what we don't like."

The groom? I wanted to say, but kept the thought to myself.

"You seem sad," she murmured as she started to work on me.

"The plans changed. We had to move the wedding up." It was a reasonable explanation. Under other circumstances, it might have been true.

Camille's eyes darted down and it took me a second to realize what she was doing.

"I'm not pregnant," I said quickly. No doubt that's what everyone assumed—and if Spencer had his way it wouldn't be long before it was true. "His grandfather passed away and he wanted to get married sooner."

"Happiness to ease the sadness," she said, her eyes wide with sympathy.

I wished I could look at it that way, but I was in the unfortunate position of knowing the real reason

Spencer wanted to marry quickly. Still, pretending it was the case to Camille was good practice. She wouldn't be the last person who attributed better motives to our hasty marriage. I needed to get used to that.

She had just placed the last pin in my hair when someone knocked softly at the door.

"We're almost ready," I called. All that was left was to slip on the gown and cape.

"It's me," Iris said, her voice muffled by the heavy door. "May I come in?"

Since I'd moved out of Willoughby Place, the only time I saw her was when she came to help with the wedding. Since a small country had been hired to produce this event on a tight timeline, it was easy enough to avoid her. I hadn't asked her to come today. Caroline must have told her. Spencer's mother had a keen eye for spotting tension between people and exploiting it. I shouldn't be surprised that she'd pulled this stunt.

"Yes," I said finally. Standing, I smoothed my silk robe over my lace corset. I didn't bother to look in the mirror. I wasn't curious what Camille had done to my hair or make-up. I knew it would be stunning, but I also knew it was a sham.

Iris stepped inside carrying a heavy dress bag. I looked at it curiously.

"I have a surprise for you," she confessed as she unzipped it. "We weren't sure there would be time, so we didn't want to say anything. You've had enough disappointment the last few weeks."

Inside was my wedding dress. The impossible dress. The dream dress. The dress I never wanted to see again in my life. I choked back a sob. Iris understandably misunderstood my reaction.

"Your wedding is going to be beautiful," she said, wrapping an arm around my shoulder and squeezing. "You deserve to have it all."

I couldn't bring myself to speak, so I allowed everyone to think I was too emotional for words. I felt numb as I slipped off my robe and they began helping me into the gown.

It fit perfectly. Iris spun me around to look in the mirror.

"Don't cry," Camille said, reaching over to dab my eyes with a handkerchief. "You'll ruin your mascara."

"Just like a princess," Iris said, her eyes watching me in the mirror.

I could only nod.

I SMILED WHEN THE PHOTOGRAPHER TOLD ME TO, but nothing I did seemed to make her happy. She huffed about the solarium, adjusting my hands, my body. I got the impression she was on the verge of asking Camille to put on the dress and pose for me when her team yelled at newcomer.

"You can't see the bride," Camille cried. "It's bad luck."

"Don't worry, sweetheart. I'm not the lucky man meeting her at the altar." Holden shot her a charming smile, but my heart flipped instead. "I just came to see how things are going."

"Terrible," the photographer announced. "I never met a stiffer bride. She's like a corpse."

"But unlike a corpse, I can hear you," I reminded her with narrowed eyes.

"It sounds like you need a drink," Holden said to me. "In fact, maybe you should take a break."

The photographer stared daggers at him but finally shrugged. She lifted her camera over her shoulders. "I'm grabbing a smoke."

It turned out that everyone else smoked, and given how stressful this whole morning had been, I couldn't blame them.

"How about that drink?" Holden asked.

"I don't think that's a good idea," I said softly.

"I'll behave." He cleared his throat, glancing down at his shoes. "Plus, I miss you. I guess we won't have many chances to be alone."

We hadn't had many lately. Despite Spencer's nonchalance about the idea of Holden serving as my captive entertainment, there was always someone around. Usually, I was grateful for the presence of others. I couldn't bear the thought of being one person in public and hiding him in private. That meant I wasn't just relying on others to keep us on our best behavior, I was also avoiding him.

"It's just that I have to do this photoshoot," I hedged.

"Yeah, and it looks like it's going swimmingly." He stared at me, silently daring me to challenge him again.

"Fine. One drink. That's it."

"Deal."

We left the solarium and made our way to the billiards room.

"You must really love pool," I teased as he uncapped a bottle of Scotch and poured some into two glasses.

"No one comes here," he said. "I really love that."

"It's unfortunate." I twiddled a crystal on my dress.

"What?" he asked, passing me a glass.

"I know your secret."

"Dirty girl, I have no secrets from you." He took a sip of his drink.

My cheeks burned, and his jaw clenched.

"Fuck." he turned his head away from me.

"What?" I asked, wishing I had a mirror.

"When you flush like that, it makes me think of what you look like..."

"Oh?" I tilted my head waiting for him to finish, and then it dawned on me. "*Oh!* I'm sorry."

"Don't be," he said gruffly. "Don't ever be sorry for that." His gaze raked over me, and he took a deep breath. "You're a goddess. Is there a goddess of brides?"

I wet my lip with my tongue, my mouth feeling a little dry under his watchful eyes. "I don't think so."

"Good," he said, taking another swig from his drink. "You're the only bride that should be worshipped."

I gulped at the implication of his words. Under my skirt, I pressed my thighs together, grateful that he couldn't see the movement. But his words were like a drug, and I felt my own inhibitions lifting.

"There's something you should know," I said softly. "I have to marry Spencer."

His throat slid as he finished his drink. He reached for the bottle and poured another.

"But I don't want to," I confessed.

"Last I checked, you could walk away. Some of us aren't so lucky," Holden said bitterly. He reached for the bottle again, but my hand flew to catch his before he had another.

"I can't do that. I want you to understand." I quickly filled him in on the uncertainty surrounding my mother's death and his grandfather's role in keeping it quiet.

"So my grandfather bought his favored son a homicidal wife. Interesting choice." His lips twitched as he spoke.

"There's no proof that I—"

"Hey," he stopped me. "I know you didn't do it. You would never."

"But as long as I don't know what happened, he

can hold this over me," I said miserably. "He threatened my whole family, and then there's his stupid contract."

"The prenup?" Holden said.

"Yes, I can't believe he thinks he can force me to..." I caught myself before I let it slip how much of my life was planned out for me.

"To do what, dirty girl?"

"Nothing."

Holden pressed a finger to my chin and tipped my face up. "What?"

"I've agreed to stop all contraception after the wedding."

I couldn't bring myself to say the rest, but judging from the anger contorting Holden's face, he had filled in the blanks.

"I guess I was wrong about why he asked me to move in. I thought he wanted to keep an eye on us, but I suppose he wants to rub salt in the wound." He fell silent, and then he raised his fist and smashed it against the bar top.

"Holden," I shrieked. "It doesn't matter."

"It does," he growled. "First, I have to see you in this dress looking like every fantasy I've ever had, and then he's going to get you pregnant and force me to watch you carry his child."

"I didn't realize..."

"What?" he demanded. "You didn't think it would bother me? I'm fucking human, Kerrigan. The thought of seeing you pregnant with his baby..." He fell silent.

I waited, trying to decide if I should tell him the worst of it and wondering how he would react. "He expects us to sleep together," I blurted out. "No matter how much I deny it, he just knows there's something between us. When I signed the contract, he said it didn't matter to him if I fucked you as long as I followed his timeline and kept it quiet."

"He wouldn't care if it wasn't his—"

"You're twins," I repeated the rationale that Spencer had given me.

Holden's shoulders shook, and for a second, I thought he was crying. Then I realized it was laughter.

"Holden?"

"I can't decide if he's doing this because he thinks we'll be okay with it or if he just really hates me." He chuckled as he looked at me, his eyes dilated from the alcohol. "What do you think?"

"I can't...I'm sorry," I said in a hushed voice.

"I know." He lifted a hand and brushed it down my cheek. "Me either."

"What are we going to do?" I asked him, my voice cracking.

"No crying," he instructed me. "I think that photographer might kill me if I brought you back with ruined make-up."

I rolled my eyes, momentarily distracted by the immediate pressure of the photoshoot. "I should have another drink and loosen up."

"Just smile," he said harshly. "You'll look gorgeous no matter what."

"Apparently not." I reached for my glass. "It's this fucking dress."

He looked down at it, then back to me, his eyes sparkling. "What's wrong with it? You're perfect. I thought that since the first time I saw it on you."

I'd forgotten that Holden had interrupted my gown shopping to deliver a message. My body heated as I recalled the way he'd looked at me that day.

"That's the problem," I admitted. "It's perfect. It's my dream dress. And I'll never wear it..."

For you. I let the words die on my lips, knowing I couldn't take them back.

"Never wear it?" he prompted in a silky voice.

I took a deep breath and found my courage. "I'll never wear it for you."

Holden inhaled sharply and our eyes locked.

"You're wearing it now," he pointed out.

"For a photoshoot," I said miserably.

"Take the picture for me," he said suddenly. "Wear the dress today for me."

I caught my lip in my teeth and nodded.

His thumb strayed over and tugged my lower lip free. "I have an idea of how to get you to loosen up."

"Holden, I... you'll ruin my make-up," I said feebly, already lost to the idea of his touch.

"No, I won't," he said wickedly. Getting to his feet, he picked me up and carried me to the pool table.

Laying my back on it, he let my legs dangle over the side. Then, he gathered my skirt and drew it slowly up to my waist. I couldn't see him past the tulle and lace, but I gasped when he kissed my inner thigh. "Take the picture for me," he coaxed. "Looking like temptation with those flushed cheeks."

I groaned as his mouth made its way to the apex of my thighs. He sucked my swollen lips through the lace of my knickers until I was trembling.

"See?" he whispered, his words dancing along my sensitive flesh. "You're wearing this dress for me now." A finger pushed away the lace barrier and his mouth covered me entirely. I arched, pleasure pulsing through me as his tongue stroked me to release.

My hands sought purchase on the felt fabric but in the end, he undid me with his tongue, leaving me a boneless heap on the billiards table. When he got to his feet, he reverently lowered the gown back over my legs.

"Now you'll always think of me when you wear this dress." He slid a hand under my back and lifted me, leaning to capture my mouth with his own. His lips moved slowly and when I began to lose control, he pulled away. "We don't want to mess up your lipstick."

As if his words were a summons, Camille's melodic voice called from the hallway. "Kerrigan? I think we need to get started."

"Fuck." Holden helped me to my feet and I smoothed the skirt as best I could. Holden dabbed at a smudge of lipstick at the corner of my mouth. The door opened and we moved quickly away from each other. By the time Camille looked inside, he was back in his spot at the bar with a fresh drink in hand.

"Are you ready to try again?" Her eyes scanned the room suspiciously.

"Yes, I think the Scotch did the trick." I smiled brightly, feeling lighter than I had all day. I would do as Holden asked. I would wear this dress for him and capture the joy he'd given me.

Camille and I made our way into the hall. We'd only gone a few steps, when she stopped me.

"Hold on," she said quietly, stepping behind me.

I froze when she began to swiftly re-pin my hair.

"There," she said with a secretive smile. "Some curls came loose."

"Oh," I feigned surprise as she inspected my make-up.

"Do I need a touch up?" I asked, hoping she didn't notice the strain in my voice.

"No." She shook her head. "You're glowing like a bride should."

"Camille..." I searched for an explanation, but she winked at me.

"Every girl must have her secrets," she said.

I nodded and followed her back to the solarium, leaving my biggest secret behind me.

"I can't believe you didn't have a hen party," Eliza whined as she lay splayed across my bed.

I shrugged, doing my best to look like I didn't care. "There wasn't time."

"Because Spencer couldn't wait to put a ring on it?" she teased. "Not that I can blame him."

"Everything just happened so fast," I said.

Eliza had arrived the night before, just in time for the wedding. Despite my insistence that she let me continue to send her rent, she refused. That meant she'd had to take every shift she could, so she could afford to come for the wedding. Thankfully, she let me pay for her bridesmaid dress. I suspected she would faint if she knew how much the designer gown cost, even off-the-rack. In return, she'd been relentlessly cheerful, since she arrived, delivering constant reassurance rather than her usual tough love.

We hadn't talked much since the DNA results confirmed I was Kerrigan. But if she was weirded out by them, she was doing a good job covering it. Other than the occasional teasing, she treated me exactly like she had in West Bexby.

It was a relief to feel normal again.

"I just feel as though I failed you." She fiddled with the tassel of a throw pillow. "You're getting married without a proper send-off."

I didn't want to know what Eliza considered an appropriate farewell to single life.

"It's not like you could have come to a hen party anyway," I pointed out.

"I would have found a way. Someone to cover my shift, bribery, human cloning. I will never shirk my best friend duties again. Whatever it takes. I'm there for you, girl."

I cracked a smile as I considered everything Eliza had done for me in the last year.

"So, your mouth can still form smiles," she said, sitting up and clutching the pillow. "I was beginning to get worried."

Maybe I was in for some tough love, after all.

"I'm just stressed out," I lied.

"That stress wouldn't have anything to do with finding out that you're actually a billionaire and that this fake wedding is real?"

So much for being a cheerleader, but I couldn't blame her. How she'd managed to avoid the topic this long was a mystery. It was all I could think about, especially with the wedding only hours away.

But I still dodged her question and pretended to inspect my dress. My cheeks warmed as I recalled Holden's face pressed between my thighs, hidden in the cloud of tulle pushed up to my waist. I hadn't seen him since that afternoon in the billiards room. I had no idea how I would face him today.

Eliza heaved a sigh when I continued to ignore her. "Okay, I didn't want to pull this card, but since you didn't have a hen party, I am forced to ask you what the hell is going on? Are you knocked up?"

"Not you, too!" I groaned, rolling my eyes. I waved a hand over my stomach. "No baby on board."

"Thank God. You're way too young for that."

If she only knew. I couldn't risk bringing the topic up now, not on my wedding day. I was having a hard enough time processing what was about to happen without worrying about the contract I'd signed. By tomorrow everything would change. I would be Kerrigan Belmond Byrd, newly married, recently blackmailed, and fresh off The Pill. It was a lot to digest and if I got too far ahead of myself, I wasn't sure I could go through with marrying Spencer.

But Eliza was having none of that. "So if it's not a shotgun wedding, why are you rushing to the altar?"

"No reason," I told her.

"Just bored? Is this what billionaires do when they tire of counting their money? Get married to shake things up?" Despite her smirk, I sensed she wasn't going to drop this.

"Spencer was ready to get married now. He has to take his grandfather's title soon and he wanted to be married before then. Like I said, not a big deal."

"But what about you?" she pressed. "Are you ready? Is this what you want?"

I reached for the diamond teardrops I planned to wear for the ceremony and poked one through my ear. "It's just like Tod said. It's an arranged marriage. I'm sure that eventually we'll smooth everything out and be perfectly happy."

"Wow." Eliza was staring at me in the mirror, her eyes popping open. "You hate him."

"I do not hate him Spencer," I hissed.

"You *really* hate him," she repeated. "What did he do? Sleep with another woman?"

"Nothing like that. It's not that I hate him —"

"Except that you do," she interjected.

I ignored her and continued, "Honestly, it has nothing to do with him."

Eliza watched me thoughtfully, and I saw the wheels in her head spinning. "Are you sure I can't smoke in here?"

I breathed a sigh of relief that she had changed the subject. "No, but we can go out on the mezzanine."

We had a little while before I needed to be dressed and ready for more photos.

"You look so beautiful," Eliza said, stopping to

admire the bridal portrait that had been placed on display in the foyer.

"Thanks." I couldn't bring myself to look at it.

"Hey, seriously." Eliza grabbed my shoulders and turned me to face the photo.

I cringed when I came face-to-face with the life-size portrait.

"You look so happy," she murmured.

I did look happy, but only I knew why my cheeks were flushed and my body relaxed and light. I'd done as Holden requested. I'd taken the picture for him, commemorating our final stolen moments before I promised to forsake all others, even him. Had he seen it yet? Did he actually want to?

A small collection of cigarette butts had collected in the corner of the second floor mezzanine, its number growing with each hour Eliza spent at Sparrow Court. We stepped into the autumn air. A crisp wind bit at our noses. Winter was already on its way. By the time we returned from our short honeymoon, the holidays would be here.

I tied my silk robe tighter around me, shivering a little in the brisk air. Eliza was wearing one in pink silk, a gift for the bridesmaids, courtesy of Iris. I'd completely sucked at being a bride and thinking of things like that.

My maid of honor lit a cigarette and took a long drag.

"So out with it," she said. "You're acting like it's

your funeral, not your wedding day. What's up? Other than you hating Spencer."

"It's not him."

"You are going to stick to that story, huh?" She tapped ash over the side of the railing, earning an annoyed look from the florist, who was busy finishing flower arrangements for the reception. Despite the rudeness of the event, the Byrds expected hundreds of people to attend. The plan was to get married in the ballroom and then host a cocktail hour on the veranda. A number of space heaters had been erected for the occasion to counter the chill. The location allowed time to convert the ballroom back for the reception. Caroline and Iris had gone over the schedule with me a thousand times. I had it memorized. But watching as the florist tucked white roses into a garland draped along the stone railing, none of it felt real.

"Can you believe this is actually happening?" Eliza said as if she could read my mind.

"No," I murmured.

"I mean, a couple of months ago you were the shittiest waitress in West Bexby." She grinned when I flashed her scathing look. "The truth hurts, babe. But now you're marrying the future Prime Minister."

"Don't remind me," I said miserably.

Eliza whirled around and grabbed me by the shoulders, stamping one foot in a mini temper tantrum. "That's it. Tell me what's going on now."

"I don't know where to start."

"Let's start with why you look like I just kicked your puppy," she suggested.

"Is that a euphemism?"

"A euphemism for what?"

"Never mind." I shook my head, knowing there wasn't time to tell her everything. I hit the major points. Eliza listened, her eyes growing wider with each passing detail. When I reached the point where I went to bed with both of them, she clapped a hand over her mouth and danced in place like she needed the loo.

"You okay there?"

"Fine," she gasped. "Go on."

By the time I caught her up on all the important parts, she'd fallen into stunned silence.

"Why didn't you tell me any of this was going on?"

"You knew about the DNA test," I said. "The rest just felt less important."

"Yeah, but you've been dealing with a lot. You should have called."

I knew that, but part of me had been scared that she would see me differently after my identity was confirmed.. "I didn't want to dump this on you," I admitted. "There's still so much I don't know."

"You should have made that therapist do the hypnosis," she decided. "I mean, what if he did and you found out that it really was an accident — would you still be marrying Spencer?"

"I don't think it matters to Spencer whether it was an accident or not." I'd consider the same question myself, but I kept coming to the same conclusion. Spencer was only interested in one thing: winning. Admitting defeat wasn't in his nature. But deep down I knew that something darker drove him. He wouldn't lose me to Holden. His brother was his best friend and his fiercest rival. He would do everything in his power to prevent that from happening. There was no chance of escaping this arrangement. He'd meant his threats to come after my family, and now on the cusp of taking his seat in parliament, he had the means to do so.

The door to the mezzanine opened, and Iris poked her head out. "There you are." She waved a hand over her face to clear a billow of smoke wafting toward her.

"Oh! I'm sorry!" Eliza dropped the cigarette butt onto her pile and put it out with her slipper.

"I was in the ballet," Iris said dismissively. "Everyone smoked."

"In that case, do you want one?" Eliza asked wickedly.

Iris pressed her lips together and then to my surprise, she nodded her head. She stepped onto the mezzanine, wearing her own pink robe. She wasn't technically a bridesmaid, but when she'd mentioned the robes, I demanded she order one for herself. Things were still strained between us but I needed her on my side. Caroline had assured me that many of my acquaintances from university would be in attendance. Considering that I couldn't remember them, it didn't mean much to me.

In the end, despite her objections, I insisted on a small bridal party. Eliza and Evie would serve as my bridesmaids. There was no need for anyone else. Spencer had backed up my wishes, opting for only his brother and a friend of his from school to be his groomsmen.

I watched, feeling a little jealous, as Iris took a cigarette from Eliza.

"Are you sure you don't want one?" Eliza asked, dangling the pack.

"Don't corrupt her," Iris cried.

"We wouldn't want that," Eliza said with a sly look in my direction.

Thankfully, Iris missed it. She inhaled and then blew a thin stream of smoke from her lips. "I have to say that after this, I'm really glad that I eloped," she confessed. "It's a madhouse around here."

She took one look at my face and backpedaled. "But everything will be fine. You don't need to worry about anything."

"I'm not worried." Not for any normal reason, at least. I didn't tell her my dearest wish was that a meteor would fall on the house and cancel the entire blessed event.

"You're going to have your hands full with that mother-in-law," she confided in me. "I think she's going to have a heart attack before the end of the day."

"Let's hope so," I muttered. Eliza elbowed me in the ribs and shot me a look. "I'm just kidding."

"She's flying around in a panic. Someone canceled and she needs someone to fill in," Iris said. "Honestly, I left before she could drag me into it."

"That's always a good policy." My eyes stayed on the caterers and florists and various help flitting in and out of the building. When I turned back to my friends, Iris was watching me intently. She dropped her cigarette and put it out with her shoe before linking her arm through mine. "Come on."

"Where are we going?" I asked as she led me inside. "You look like you could use a drink," she said.

"Yeah she could," Eliza said. I shot her a warning look and she pretended to zip her mouth closed.

"Is there something wrong?" Iris asked, catching the gesture.

"I'm just nervous." That was true. But I knew it was more than the usual bridal worries. I was nervous about being bound to Spencer Byrd for the rest of my life. I was nervous about the expectations he had for me. My mind strayed to the contract I had signed. If it meant protecting the people I loved, I would sign it again. But that didn't make what I was about to do any easier.

We returned to my room, and I was surprised to find a bucket filled with ice and champagne.

"Perfect!" Eliza said, taking it from the bucket.

"Caroline must have sent it upstairs." Iris picked up the small card sitting in front of the ice bucket, but she refrained from opening it.

"That sounds way too friendly for her," I said.

"You're marrying her son. Give it time."

My eyes strayed to the wedding dress hanging in the closet. "But if I decide to wear the other dress?"

"What?" Iris asked, absently.

"I think I like the other dress more."

"But you love this dress," she said slowly.

"The fur will look better given the weather." It was a feeble lie at best, but Iris sighed.

"I can send someone to get it for you."

"Don't worry about it," I said, trying to swallow the lump of tears forming in my throat.

"Kerrigan, are you sure —"

The door burst open, interrupting her, and Evie rushed inside, her blonde curls bouncing around her shoulders, half of her hair still in rollers. She was wearing her pink bridesmaid robe and she looked flushed like she had run across the house to reach me.

"What's wrong?" I asked her when I saw the look on her face.

"It's Holden," she said.

"What about him?" My heart skipped a beat and then stopped altogether when she told me, "He took off. He's not coming to the wedding."

CHAPTER THIRTY

Iris gasped and rushed toward the door, abandoning the champagne on a side table. "That must be what has made Caroline so upset. I should go check on her."

I nodded, my whole body going numb. She left to calm the mother of the groom, but I stood there. Meanwhile, Eliza badgered Evie for information.

"He was supposed to take Spencer for his stag night," Evie told her in a conspiratorial voice, "but then he canceled last minute."

"Why doesn't it surprise me that there wasn't time for you to have a hen night but there was time for Spencer to have a stag night?" Eliza said bitterly.

"I didn't want a hen party," I told her, "and you know why."

Evie looked at both of us in turn, curiosity peaking on her face.

"There was no point. I only have one bridesmaid that can go to a bar," I lied.

"Okay," Evie said, but I could tell she wasn't buying it.

"What happened? Why did he cancel? Where did he go?" Eliza asked, steering the conversation back to the topic of Holden.

I was going to be sick. Their voices faded as I made my way to the corner chair and sank slowly into it. It didn't matter where he'd gone. He wasn't here. Spencer would be furious, and the blame for his disappearance would fall squarely on my shoulders. That wasn't what bothered me. It was the guilt I felt for being glad I wouldn't have to face Holden as I said my vows to Spencer.

"Mom thinks that he had a fight with Spencer, and he took off. He does things like that," Evie said sadly. I noticed that she didn't look at me as she spoke. Did she suspect the truth?

No one would be surprised that the brothers got into a fight, even on one's wedding day. It was an easy story to swallow. That might be what they wanted to believe, but I knew the truth. This wasn't about Spencer. This was about me.

I stared out the window. A hedge blocked the view past Sparrow Court. As far as I could tell from here, the outside world didn't exist. Of course, that was the entire point. It was the Byrd family's personal kingdom and my beautiful cage.

"Hey," Eliza said softly, interrupting my melancholy. "Read this." She handed me the card that had arrived with the champagne.

I took it with trembling hands and read the four words written on it. I looked up at her, choking back a sob.

Next time, dirty girl.

There wouldn't be a next time. He was gone. I was getting married. It wasn't a promise. It was a farewell.

"That's what I thought," she muttered.

"What does it say?" Evie strained to read the card, but I pressed it to my chest out of her view.

"Believe me, you don't want to know," Eliza told her.

"This isn't about Spencer, is it? Holden left because of you," she said, but her tone was free of any judgment.

"You shouldn't worry about it," I said softly. I folded the card in half and tucked it into the pocket of my robe.

"Something is going on between you two."

She waited for me to deny it, but I didn't have the energy. Not anymore.

"Don't marry Spencer," she blurted out.

Eliza and I both stared at her. I was shocked, but Eliza looked impressed.

"He's a jerk. Not always, but enough of the time," she amended quickly as if she was afraid to even consider criticizing him. "He doesn't deserve you and you clearly have feelings for my brother. Holden, I mean. And I think he loves you, too. So why marry Spencer. All of you will be miserable and that will make me miserable, too. If that's —"

"Evie, hold your tongue," Caroline said sharply. We turned to find her glaring at her only daughter from the doorway. She shifted in her heels, already dressed for the ceremony, and did her best to look casual. "Your opinion is unwanted." She turned her attention to me. "I assume Evie has told you that Holden won't be joining us for the wedding."

I nodded, blood roaring in my ears as I wondered how much of Evie's speech she had heard. Probably none of it, Caroline appeared to filter out unpleasant truths. She had turned a blind eye to my relationship with her sons since we'd been introduced.

"Thankfully, Spencer has a cousin in attendance. He's going to step in, and no one will be any the wiser."

"You don't think people will think it's weird that Holden isn't here?" Evie demanded, planting a hand on her hip.

"I don't really care what people think," her mother spit back.

"Since when?" Immediately, Evie clapped a hand over her mouth, realizing what she said.

"I think you better finish getting ready," her mother said coldly. Then she looked at me. "As should you. It's your wedding day. Focus on that."

"Maybe we should wait." It spilled out of my mouth before I realized it was on my tongue.

Caroline had already begun to turn toward the hall and she froze for a moment. Then, she swiveled slowly back, a look of pure hatred on her face. "And why would we do that?"

"Spencer should have his brother here," I said.

"Is that the only reason?" she said meaningfully. She was baiting me, but when I didn't bite, she dangled the hook. "I don't think Spencer will miss his brother at all. I think you will."

CHAPTER THIRTY-ONE

I was too shocked to say anything.

Her eyes sparkled over her win. "I need to see to the final preparations. Evie, get dressed!"

None of us spoke as she sashayed out of sight.

"She's really mad at me, huh?" Evie broke the silence.

"Welcome to the club."

"We should get matching shirts," Evie said glumly.

I hated that Evie had gotten dragged into all of this. Almost as much as I hated Caroline for the way she treated her daughter. I pushed onto my feet and wrapped an arm around Evie's shoulders.

"I know everything is crazy right now," I admitted, "and I don't expect you to understand all of it, but I want you to know that I'm really glad that you're going to be my sister."

Tears filled her eyes, and she squeaked, "Really?"

"*Really.*" I meant it. Maybe life wouldn't turn out the way I planned, but I would find happiness where I could. Today, I was losing a piece of myself, but I was gaining something, too. There was a bright side, and I clung to it.

"I better go get ready," Evie said. "Before mom kills me."

I nodded and watched her leave.

"I guess I should get dressed," I said in a hollow voice.

"Maybe—"

I cut Eliza off with a sharp look.

"It's too late," I said firmly. "This is happening."

She didn't debate me, but when she went to the closet to retrieve the other gown, I stopped her.

"I'm going to wear the dress," I said.

"Are you sure?"

Yes. Wearing the dream dress didn't change anything. Eliza had said I looked like it was my funeral, not my wedding day before. Now I saw the truth in that. Today was my funeral. I would walk down the aisle, say my vows, and Kerrigan Belmond would be gone forever. If I was going to die, I would do it in the beautiful dress. I would remember how Holden's eyes lit up when he saw me in it. I would linger in the moments we'd stolen together while I wore it. It wasn't my wedding dress. It was my shroud.

Eliza helped me into the gown, taking care not to ruin my hair or make-up. Camille would check in soon to see if I needed any touch-ups, but as I looked in the mirror, I saw what the world would see. A perfect bride on her perfect day.

The lie was packaged and ready to deliver.

There was only one thing to do. I picked up the bottle of champagne and popped the cork.

"Do you think this is enough to get us drunk?" I asked as bubbles fizzed out the top.

Eliza didn't respond. I looked up, blinking through my own tears, and found her staring at me. But she didn't look sad or concerned, she was thinking.

"What is it?" I asked.

"Your therapist," she said, her eyes darting around the room like she was moving invisible pieces into place. "What did he say about the panic attacks?"

"Why does that matter?" I had no idea why she had come back to this after everything I had confessed to her.

"Just tell me," Eliza said impatiently.

"He said I should give into them or something," I said, searching my memory for exactly how Dr. Simmons had put it. "It doesn't really matter, though, I haven't had one in days. I've been on the verge of one a couple of times, but I managed to stay in control."

"Yeah, that's the problem," she said, sounding a bit too excited. "You won't let yourself have one."

"I hardly see how that's a problem," I said dryly. The last thing I needed was to pass out on the day of my wedding. Spencer would probably marry me regardless of my state of consciousness.

"Don't you see? You said it yourself. You want to know the truth." She bounced on her feet. "That's what he was trying to tell you. You have to give in to the attack."

"I don't see how it's going to help," I asked.

"He said it was like drowning, right?"

I nodded.

"And he said he thought it had something to do with your mother's death, right? Like it was a reaction to the trauma," she continued.

"I'm sure it does. What's more traumatic than that?"

"What if it's your memories?" she asked. "What if you're trying to remember? I mean if that's where the trauma started, isn't that where your memories got stuck? What if you could remember?"

I stared at her before slowly shaking my head. "It's too late for that."

"Like hell it is." Eliza marched to the door and slammed it shut. She turned and pressed her body against it like a human barrier. "Holden left because he's in love with you, and he couldn't stand to see you get married."

My head spun at the u-turn her thoughts had taken.

"I'm aware of that," I said in a flat voice.

"And it doesn't matter what dress you wear,

you're marrying the wrong brother today," she continued, giving a voice to the terrible thoughts in my head.

"Eliza, this isn't helping —"

"And you are going to become exactly the thing you tried to run away from," she said, ignoring me. "Spencer is going to control you. He's going to force you to have babies. He's going to force you to smile and stand by his side. He's going to lock you away in this house to rot, and *he is never going to love you.*"

Her words ran through me like ice. I wrapped my arms around myself fighting the sudden chill in the room. "What are you doing?"

"What if the authorities were right? What if your mother's death wasn't an accident?"

"Then hat means that I—"

"I'm not saying you killed her," she cut me off.

"What are you saying?" I cried. Before she could respond a wave hit me from the side, crashed over me, and I swayed on my feet. Darkness tugged at the edge of my vision. Stumbling, I grabbed the bed to keep from falling. "Stop!"

"You saw it. You survived it."

I turned pleading eyes on her.

But she delivered the final blow with deft precision. "What kind of a daughter leaves her mother to drown?"

The current pulled me under. Blackness swallowed me. I tried to fight it. Somewhere, in the distance, Eliza's voice called to me, "Give in. You're strong enough to face it."

But I was drowning. I opened my mouth to tell her, and water rushed down my throat. It was too strong for me. I couldn't see as the riptide pushed and pulled me under in the water's onyx surface. Night had fallen early this evening, and the world was never darker than on open water. I tried to push myself up toward the air, but I bumped into something as soon as I kicked. Spinning with the little strength I had left, I spun to find my mother's lifeless body. The whites of her eyes stared back at me with unseeing determination. I opened my mouth to scream and water burned in my lungs. I clamped it shut and grabbed hold of her around the waist. I wouldn't die like this, but I wouldn't leave her either. But she spasmed, her mouth snapping open. Bubbles escaped as she swallowed a mouthful of water. I lost hold of her as her eyes blinked. She was alive. There was still time. In the black water, she was a pale ghost, but she was alive. Her hand closed around my arm and I started to pull us up to safety.

But she resisted.

No, she fought me. My mother gripped my arm and dragged me deeper down.

Down.

Down.

Into the darkness.

Into the abyss.

Into nothing itself.

Instinct took over. I kicked my legs, lashing out and catching her in the chest with my foot. It was enough to break her hold, and she released me. Before she could grab me again, I pushed with all of my strength toward the surface.

Toward my life.

Toward the world.

Toward myself.

She sank beneath me, her white summer dress floating around her as she gave herself to the ocean. And as I broke through the waves, gasping for air, all I could see was the last glimpse of regret in her eyes.

Our vessel had drifted in the strong tide, and I found myself, bobbing up and down in the open water, midway between the shore and the yacht. I had to swim toward one. The yacht might be slightly closer, But I couldn't bring myself to look at it. Not after what had happened. There was no safety in its direction, and I wanted to leave its memories unvisited. I didn't want to remember laughing with my mother while drinking an illicit bottle of wine and listening to her sad stories of lost loves.

Going back to the yacht now would force me to relive those final moments. It would force me to accept the moment she wrapped her arms around me. I hugged her back and she held me tightly before she dragged us both over the side of the boat.

CHAPTER THIRTY-TWO

I crumbled to the ground, my hands scraping the Persian rug beneath me. I dug my nails into it, gripping it as though my life depended on it. The burning in my lungs vanished, and I gulped cool air. The ocean was gone, but my memories remained. I was back in my room in Sparrow Court, my wedding gown pooled around me, but I wasn't any safer.

"Are you okay?" Eliza said soothingly as she knelt beside me. "You were yelling. I couldn't understand half of it."

I looked up at her, realizing the moisture on my face wasn't from the water that had overtaken me, but my own tears. It had been a panic attack. I'd been here the whole time. Nothing about it, but the memories were real. "I know what happened," I whispered. "It wasn't me. I didn't kill her. At least, not really."

"You don't have to tell me," Eliza said.

But I was afraid it would slip away like a dream. I shook my head. "I want to while I can still remember it."

I told her what I remembered. I told her about the flashes of memory that I'd had from the boat. How my mother had told me about the love she lost and warned me that someday someone would break my heart. "We were drinking wine. I didn't think anything of it," I said, startled to realize how blind I had been to my mother's mood. "She never let me do things like that."

"So she was drunk," Eliza said, "and that's why the accident happened."

I shook my head, a lump forming in my throat. I wasn't sure if I could really admit the truth.

"Kerrigan?"

"It wasn't an accident," I said so quietly that I wasn't sure she heard me. "She pulled us into the water."

"Pulled?" she repeated with shock.

I nodded, unable to process it all myself.

"Why would she do that?" Eliza sat back on her heels in a daze. "Why would she try to drown you?"

"I think she was trying to save me."

"Save you from what?" Eliza tilted her head, and I knew I wasn't making sense to her. I barely understood it myself.

"From this," I said, finally realizing why I had run. "This life destroyed her. The love she told me about that night wasn't my father, but a man her parents didn't approve of her marrying. They forced her to end it and demanded she marry Tod. She was terrified of their disapproval."

Had she known the same fate would befall me someday? Or was she just too sad and worn down to fight the darkness any longer?

I tried to imagine how anyone could feel that desperate like they had no other choice, and I realized with startling clarity, that I didn't have to imagine at all. I was living it now.

"You can't marry Spencer," Eliza said. She stood and walked toward the door.

Her movement broke me free of the spell the memories had cast over me. "What are you doing?"

"I'm going to find Iris, and she is going to listen to you, and then you're going to call the wedding off," Eliza said firmly.

I stared at her, wondering which one of us was making less sense.

"I can't do that," I said when she fixed me her eyes on me, determination etched on her face. "It doesn't matter what the truth is. Spencer doesn't care. If I call off the wedding, he will ruin everyone's lives."

Eliza opened her mouth to argue with me, but Iris stepped into the room and spoke for her. "Is it any better to ruin yours?" She shook her head sadly. "Kerrigan, I don't know why you believe you have to marry Spencer, but let me be clear, you don't have to do anything you don't want to do."

They were easy words to say, but I knew the cost of following through. They had to listen to me.

"You don't understand. It's the only way to protect you. The only way to protect..." I choked on Holden's name. I buried my face in my hands, confusion churning through me.

"What about you?" Eliza asked. "What if it ruins you like it did your mother? What will you do when your child faces the same arrangement?"

Her words struck me like a bullet, knocking the wind out of me. For a moment, I couldn't speak and when I finally found my voice, it was brittle. "I'm not strong enough."

Iris bent and looked me in the eye. "Queens hold all the power."

Her words settled over the wound Eliza's had left. They wrapped themselves around me like a bandage, stemming the pain, and suddenly I could breathe.

"I don't want to marry Spencer."

"I'll take care of everything," Iris began.

"Don't," I stopped her. Now that I'd found my voice, I was determined to use it. She was right. Queens held all the power, and it was time to use mine. "I need to do it myself. This is my chapter to end."

CHAPTER THIRTY-THREE

The house was full of people. Everywhere I looked there were ornate flower arrangements and unlit candles. The door of the ballroom opened as I passed and I paused just long enough to see the rows of gold-lacquered chairs lined up on two sides of a spectacular walkway. An arch had been erected and draped with Japanese wisteria. The delicate, white blooms had been flown in this morning. Silk brocade lined the path to the ceremonial altar. I swallowed as I took it all in and tried not to feel guilty for what I was about to do.

I found Spencer in the solarium, hiding amongst his plants. Despite his brother's absence, it was clear Spencer had enjoyed a stag night the previous evening. Whiskey lingered on his breath, and his eyes were red. As I approached, his eyebrow quirked up.

"Isn't it bad luck to see you before the wedding?" he asked, studying me from head-to-toe. He said nothing about my dress. Despite this being his first glimpse of me, the moment held all the romance of a business transaction.

This was it. I knew what I had to do. I didn't think about the repercussions or what I wanted after this was over. This had to happen first. It was time for my real life to begin.

I lifted my chin and looked him dead in the eye. "I'm not marrying you."

"Don't be ridiculous, Kerrigan." Despite his dismissive tone, his eyes flashed as he spoke.

"I'm not marrying you," I repeated. "I've already told Iris, and she's telling everyone else. The wedding is off."

I slid the ring he'd given me off my finger. A weight lifted as soon as I took it off. It was a sign. But when I held it out to him, he refused to accept it. I waited as patiently as I could before placing the ring next to one of his beloved plants. Spencer glanced at it before turning on me.

"Let me be clear, we are getting married today," he roared.

"No, we aren't," I said in a slow, measured voice. It was easier to stay calm as he got more upset. His anger only assured me that I was making the right decision. "I'm sorry. I didn't want to hurt you."

"But you decided to humiliate me, instead. Is that

it?" He grabbed me by the wrist and yanked me to his chest. Spencer's arms bracketed my body, refusing to release me.

"Let me go." I tried to pull free, but his grip tightened.

"You belong to me. You signed the contract," he seethed, ignoring my protests. Fury showed in his eyes as he held me captive.

I fought the urge to shrink under his brutal gaze, but I held my ground. "The contract means nothing until we're married. It's just a piece of paper."

"Well, let's see about that." He dragged me toward the house. I fought him twisting in his grip. But the harder I struggled, the more force he exerted. "Have you forgotten what I can do to your family?" he growled. "You need me. It's too late to change your mind."

"I'm in love with your brother," I blurted out. I'd never admitted it to him. Until now, I'd dodged his suspicions and soothed his paranoia. But neither of us could hide from the truth any longer.

Spencer's stopped, but he didn't let me go. "You can't be."

"Pretty sure, I am," I told him. "For years."

"Years that you don't remember," he said, his face lighting with savage delight as he saw my shock. "You thought I didn't know? Tell me, who are you today: poor Kate or spoiled Kerrigan?"

"You bastard," I said, smacking my palm into his chest. "You knew the whole time?"

"Of course, I knew," he snapped. "Why did you think I delayed the engagement?"

"It was a lie," I said, seeing him for the first time. "All of it."

"Not all of it," he murmured. "I enjoyed fucking you."

My stomach heaved. I'd given this man so much. I'd let him inside. I'd lost my virginity to him. And the whole time he had been lying, building his dynasty on secrets and manipulations at the cost of my soul.

"I hate you."

"I'm not terribly fond of you at the moment," he admitted, squeezing my arm. "But you will fulfill the terms of our arrangement."

"Never."

"Why are you fighting this? I told you you could have him." Veins appeared in the side of his neck, and I wondered if he was actually restraining himself. The thought was terrifying. How much worse could this get? "The poor little rich bitch wants everything, doesn't she?"

"Not you," I said, squirming in his embrace. His fingers sank into my skin, bruising at, and I cried out. "Stop it! You're hurting me."

"You think this hurts? Walk out that door and see what I can do to you," he said with a dangerous edge.

"By the time I'm through, you will be penniless, imprisoned, and ruined. You'll regret the day you met me."

"Too late for that. I already do." I shoved him with my free arm, but he was too strong. He released me just to raise his hand to strike.

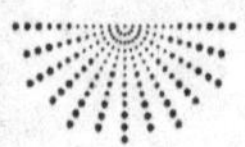

CHAPTER THIRTY-FOUR

His hand flew, and I turned my face to avoid the worst of it. But it made no contact.

"Don't you know better than to hit a lady?" Holden growled at him, and relief flooded through me. I turned to find him standing there, holding his brother's arm in place. Spencer was frozen, mid-swing.

"She's not a lady." Spencer turned his head and spit on the floor. "Isn't that what you're always saying about her? She's a dirty girl, right?"

"Spencer, you're in danger of saying something that you're going to regret," Holden warned him.

"The only thing I regret is letting that piece of trash into my—"

He didn't finish the sentence. Holden's fist knocked the words out of his mouth. Spencer crashed to the floor, staring at his brother with a dazed look.

"You've crossed the line," Spencer growled. "You want her. She's yours. You too can have each other. Enjoy being penniless on the streets with that –"

"Careful what you say about her. She might be a dirty girl, but she's *my* dirty girl," Holden stopped him.

It was possibly a very sweet thing to say, but I was too overwhelmed by the moment. I rushed toward him, but he held up a hand.

"You came back," I said.

"I never really left. Something kept me here." His throat slid as he looked at me. "God, you're beautiful."

Happiness swelled in my chest and for a moment, everything felt possible.

Then Spencer stood up. But he didn't come at either of us. Instead, he brushed dirt from his suit pants and yelled at a passing server. "You," he said.

The man stopped and waited, looking between the three of us with barely contained interest. I couldn't imagine what this looked like. "Call the police. I want these two escorted off-premises."

The man looked at me again, no doubt confused that the bride was being kicked out on her wedding day.

"Sir, I'm just a caterer," the man protested.

"I'm paying you, aren't I?" Spencer exploded.

"Don't worry about it." Holden clapped him on the shoulder, distracting him long enough for the poor guy to escape. "We were already leaving."

He reached for my hand and I knit my fingers through his. I'd made it to shore, at last. I was safe.

"You sure about this?" he whispered to me.

"Geez, let me think about it," I said dryly.

"In fairness, you can be indecisive."

I raised an eyebrow at him and he held up his other hand in surrender.

There was a shuffle of footsteps on the stone floor, and Spencer lurched toward us. Holden moved out of the way, wrapping an arm around my waist and pushing me behind him. "I think that's our cue to go." He tipped his head toward the exit. "After you."

I didn't waste any time. Lifting my skirts, I ran toward the door. Before I reached it, someone opened it from the outside and it swung wide like a cage door. I rushed toward it, my heart taking flight as I stepped into the sunlight and flew free at last.

THE DRIVEWAY WAS FULL OF CATERING VANS AND photography equipment and more than a few people stopped to stare as Holden and I raced away from the house, hand-in-hand. Considering he was wearing a pair of old jeans and a T-shirt, and I was still in my wedding dress, I understood their confusion. His Range Rover was parked near the gate, the keys in the ignition and engine running.

"Were you planning on going somewhere?" I asked as we hurried toward it.

"Not without you."

"What if I tried to stop you?"

"Why do you think I left the car running? It's better to be ready if you might need to kidnap someone." I couldn't help but smile. After everything, we had fought. For ourselves. For each other. We'd broken free on our own, so we could be together.

He rushed forward and opened the door. "Allow me."

"You aren't going to turn into a gentleman on me, are you?"

"I'd say it's unlikely," he reassured me He helped me into the passenger seat and then proceeded to stuff my skirt in as quickly as he could. We both knew that Spencer had probably made good on his promise to call the police.

"This is a lot of dress," he grumbled, barely getting it all in the cabin. He managed to shut my door. I fought the cloud of tulle, pushing it down so I could see beyond it.

Holden reached the driver's side, and my heart soared. We'd finally escaped.

"What are you doing?" Caroline shrieked, her voice slicing through the air, and my joy turned to ashes.

Holden turned around and waved to her. "Surprise, mum! I think I'm finally settling down"

"You can't do this," she said, walking swiftly

toward the car. Apparently, she was still above running. I mean, what would people think?

Holden shrugged. "I think I already did."

"That is your brother's fiancée." She jabbed a finger in my direction.

"No," he corrected her, "that is the love of my life."

"You don't even know her."

Holden didn't argue with her. Instead, he closed his door and drove toward the gate, leaving the past where it belonged. Behind us. Someday, we might have to reveal the truth. But when we were ready. Those memories belonged to us, even the ones I'd lost along the way, and we would find them together.

He stopped the car at the end of the drive and turned to me. "Are you sure about this?"

"Absolutely."

His gaze drifted out the window, and he frowned.

"What?" I asked as my pulse pounded.

"You and me." He shook his head, and I thought my heart might stop. "This is going to make family Christmas awkward."

I rolled my eyes, instantly feeling calm. After what we had survived, I knew we could make it through anything. "Want to change your mind?"

"Nah." He grinned at me, and my heart flipped as I realized this was actually happening. "You're worth the trouble. You always have been."

He leaned across the console and took my chin in his hands. A deep peace settled over me. We had the rest of our lives together, and when he brought his lips to mine, I knew we could conquer anything. As long as we did it together.

When I finally pulled away, his eyes remained closed, a smile playing on his lips. After a minute, he opened them and gestured toward the road ahead. "Where do you want to go?"

"Anywhere," I said with total certainty. I wasn't the person I'd been when I came to Sparrow Court. I was still finding the real me, but now I knew I could be whoever I wanted. And I knew exactly who I wanted by my side. "I'll go anywhere with you."

ACKNOWLEDGMENTS

To my wonderful readers, thank you for reading. Thank you for letting me tell you stories. And thank you to my friends, family, and team for making it happen. I couldn't do any of this without you.

ABOUT THE AUTHOR

GENEVA LEE is the *New York Times*, *USA Today*, and internationally bestselling author of over a dozen novels, including the Royals Saga which has sold two million copies worldwide. She lives in Poulsbo Washington with her husband and three children, and she co-owns Away With Words Bookshop with her sister.

Connect with her online at:
www.GenevaLee.com

Or on social media at:

facebook.com/Genevaleebooks

instagram.com/Realgenevalee

www.ingramcontent.com/pod-product-compliance
Lightning Source LLC
Chambersburg PA
CBHW010844190726
48286CB00012BA/2982